SELF-PORTRAIT WITH GHOST

ALSO BY MENG JIN

Little Gods

SELF-PORTRAIT WITH GHOST

short stories

MENG JIN

MARINER BOOKS

Boston   New York

FIRST EDITION

Designed by Michelle Crowe

Library of Congress Cataloging-in-Publication Data

Names: Jin, Meng, 1989- author.
Title: Self-portrait with ghost : short stories / Meng Jin.
Other titles: Self-portrait with ghost (Compilation)
Description: First edition. | Boston ; New York : Mariner Books, [2022]
Identifiers: LCCN 2022002882 (print) | LCCN 2022002883 (ebook) | ISBN 9780063160712 (hardcover) | ISBN 9780063160729 (trade paperback) | ISBN 9780063160736 (ebook)
Subjects: LCGFT: Short stories.
Classification: LCC PS3610.I56 S45 2022 (print) | LCC PS3610.I56 (ebook) | DDC 813/.6—dc23/eng/20220314
LC record available at https://lccn.loc.gov/2022002882
LC ebook record available at https://lccn.loc.gov/2022002883

ISBN 978-0-06-316071-2

22 23 24 25 26 LSC 10 9 8 7 6 5 4 3 2 1

for my mother, and the other women who made me

In my own "Painter and Model" painting, I have it all.
I am both artist and sitter. By looking at myself I don't
need to stage a drama about power; I am empowered
by the very fact that I am representing myself as I am:
a painter.

—Celia Paul, *Self-Portrait*

But the common error was to still believe that everything
could be transformed into poetry and words.

—Natalia Ginzburg, *Family Lexicon*

Contents

Phillip Is Dead

Poor man. I got the news as I was coming aboveground. "Phillip is dead," the subject line said. In the body of the email were details of the memorial.

I was shocked. Not so much because Phillip was dead but because I had not thought of him in years. "Phillip is dancing," the email might have said, or "Phillip is wearing a yellow hat." It would have been news as much to me.

Well, these words *were* different. Phillip had been as good as dead to me, for no pernicious reason. Just—irrelevance. Now he'd been resurrected and killed, in one swift blow.

I WENT HOME AND POURED a shot of scotch. I waited for my lover to come. I was in love, oh yes. Not the rapturous kind that turns and thins your sleep, but a satisfying, contented love. I woke in the mornings well-rested and warm, like a loaf of risen bread. I was still learning how to manage myself in this state. For much of my adult life, I had been sustained by a vision of doomed loneliness, a tragic fate I could run away from and toward, simultaneously. Movement was something, drive was something. But the engine I'd relied on—my lover was rendering it false.

He walked in the door. I kissed him on the mouth. It was sour from the long day, and so was mine.

"You've ruined me," I said.

He laughed; I said it all the time. "What did I do now?"

"You've made me so happy, I don't feel the need to prove anything."

"Is it such a bad thing?" he said. He tipped the drink down my throat.

I swallowed. "Not bad, no, I don't think."

WHICH IS TO SAY I was glad it was Phillip who was dead and not me. Oh, I felt a little sorry for him, sure. But mostly I felt like gloating. "How lucky I am, I'm still alive!" If Phillip were still alive, I thought, he wouldn't begrudge me this feeling. He had believed in pursuing victory with ruthless glee. He had fancied himself a Nietzschean. All this came rushing back to me, all the dumb things he'd said and believed. Once, I'd almost forgotten, he had taken credit for me:

"I made you," he'd said. Winking, but I could see he wanted to be serious. He cocked his head as if to ask, "Don't you think?"

I'd humored him. "Sure," I said. "Of course."

MY MAIN QUARREL WITH PHILLIP had been regarding the nature of humanity. To put it simply, I'd believed in goodness, and he in the opposite. Not exactly in evil—even Phillip was not so simple—but that morality, and its various manifestations, was a scam. It had been revealed to Phillip during an acid trip that the true nature of things lay in their dying. In the trees and in the dirt, in the flesh on his own hands, Phillip saw cells losing form and decaying, maggots and worms nibbling at the edges of things and bursting from their cores. He could not unsee this vision. Even when he was stone-cold sober, it would ambush him. Once, when we were fucking, he'd looked into my face as he was coming and saw my eyes pop out, dangling from their sockets, and the edges of my mouth rotting. Phillip always kept his eyes wide open while fucking.

Phillip's visions played in my head like a warning reel. For years, I feared altering my sight. I accepted the tab on my tongue only much later, when I was altered already, suffering from boredom and invincibility. I braced for death. But I saw forms shimmering beyond their boundaries, every rock and plant and breath of wind vibrating with life. Colors and shapes extended their hands to make themselves known to me. Hello, I am blue. Hello, I am a line.

"Ew," Phillip would have said. "Your *feelings*," he had said often, with disdain, of my need for beauty. He had called it my great weakness. "Your *moral* failing," he'd said, "as a person and as an artist."

We were trying to be artists. We were very young and foolish. All of us were, but Phillip and I were the worst. We lived in the same two-story house in the southwest quadrant of the city, with the rest of the young Americans. Phillip was rich, and I was too, though once I had been poor. Young, American, idealistic, we had come to the island to take classes at the national university, which in every department culminated in theoretical forms of utopianism, theories the nation believed it was realizing in practice. Really we were enacting a shared adventure of poverty, living as the locals lived, but with our reserves of cash and our promised escape. At the end of term, our special visas would expire, and a plane would shuttle us back to America. The certainty of our departure transformed what should have been tedious into experiences of meaning: the thick heat, the crumbling infrastructure, the food and power shortages.

I had opted out of the special classes in English created for the Americans. Instead I populated my schedule with punishing courses in which I was the only foreigner. Because I'd been poor, and because I had not always been American, I'd believed I was there for different reasons than the rest.

To my disappointment I was not the only American in Theory and Practice of Art. I walked into the classroom and saw Phillip slumped in the back row. I had avoided him in the house and I avoided him here, easily: boys like Phillip never noticed me. I took pride in disappearing. My skin had darkened under the island sun, and a childhood of foreignness had taught me how to become invisible, picking up ways of movement and speech unfamiliar to me. I wore the local mannerisms so successfully that one day, on a teaching rampage, the professor called on me.

"What does Nietzsche say is the difference between music and other forms of art!" he bellowed.

"That music is the direct expression of primordial truth, a rip in the fabric of appearances," I answered. I spoke slowly and deliberately. "Other art forms are merely representations of things as they are."

The professor folded his arms and squinted at me.

"You're a foreign student," he said.

I nodded. Heads in the room craned to take a better look at me.

"Where are you from?"

"The United States."

"You look Chinese! Korean? Japanese!"

"I was born in China."

He nodded with satisfaction: "Your accent is Chinese!"

"No, it is gringo."

"Sounds Chinese to me!" he said. He turned to another student. "Arnaldo! Is China correct, is primordial truth what separates Nietzsche's music from other forms of art? Explain how that applies to Tintoretto's *Ascension of Christ*!"

That day after class Phillip ran after me.

"Hey, hey!" he shouted. Phillip was unabashedly American, yellow-haired and pinking in the sun, with a loping gait that was confident and neurotic at once. "You! Wait!"

Finally he caught up to me. "So you *get* that class?" he asked. Without waiting for an answer, he fell into step beside me, speaking in loud English of his failures of comprehension at the university and generally, "in this fucking place." He was reading the texts in English and that was hard enough. He had signed up for the class thinking it was an art class, thinking we'd actually get to *practice art*, that was what the course name said, right? Because, he said with aplomb, quite literally puffing out his chest, "I'm an artist!"

I must have given something away then. He stopped talking and looked at me. "What, are you an artist too?" He paused, with apprehension or with hope. "It's okay if you aren't."

"Tell me about your art," I said instead.

"Tell me about *your* art," he shot back. I sniffed and kept walking. Phillip said, "You think I didn't notice you, and you're all tense with it, aren't you? I'm not stupid, I've seen you at dinner. I thought you were probably boring, I thought you were a little nerd. I was wrong, okay? I was wrong!"

Phillip waited for me to speak.

"Sometimes I take photographs," I offered.

"Hmm!" He looked me up and down. "Where's your camera?"

I shrugged with haughty secrecy.

"I mostly paint," Phillip said. "I'm a painter! I'll show you my paintings when we get back to the house!"

His paintings were of rot. Interested in expression, but not in beauty or technique, though they were recognizable as of a piece, the palette in blues and browns with splashes of dull green and a violent, pukey yellow. The most accomplished depicted a tree growing up and down, like a rotated Rorschach, with the branches decaying and the roots flowering, the ugliest flowers one had ever seen. "Are these meant to be ugly?" I said. "Or are you just bad?"

He shrugged. "This is how I paint." With total candor he spoke of his hallucinations: he was trying to re-create the landscape of his other consciousness. Was the concept facile or elegant, obvious or direct? Was I impressed or embarrassed for him? I didn't know, perhaps because in spite of myself I found him handsome and sure, made in the colors and dimensions I was trained to recognize as handsome and sure: white, tall, and boyishly grinning, looking right through me.

"Derivative," I said of his paintings. "Worst of all, they repulse the eye. I look at these and see 'I am a tortured artist,' and that's it. Life has beauty too, you know, and joy."

"Joy?" Phillip made a face of exaggerated disgust. "There is only power."

"Now show me your photographs," he demanded.

"No."

From then on we spent much of our time together. We disagreed about everything and Phillip liked this, liked arguing. Always I won. Because I was rigorous, relentless; I wouldn't drop it until I won. I told myself that his arguments disgusted me, that they, like Phillip, were depraved and inhumane. I construed him as an intellectual charity case, a misguided white boy I might fix or, if he was truly as hopeless as he seemed, decommission—at least declaw. But the more I went at him, the stronger he got. He liked getting flayed. He got off on the precision of my insults. When he lost, he gave exhilarated concessions, eyes wild with contempt and satisfaction, as if he had finally gained entrance into a truth of himself he knew deep down but hadn't until then had the evidence to prove.

IT WAS OKAY THAT PHILLIP was dead, I thought at the memorial. Not many would miss him. I looked into the faces of the mourners and saw that I was right. To be sure, there was plenty of shock, among the young people especially, who stood slack-jawed and gaping in the unexpected face of mortality. But peel back the veil of appropriate grief and what remained was mostly novelty. "Can you believe it?" "I can't *believe* it!" "Phillip is dead!" "My god, he's fucking *dead*!" Phillip could have gone to the moon.

The memorial was held in a cathedral, cavernous and rippled with mottled light, the kind of place I never would have guessed could exist in New York City. The location surprised me for other reasons too. Phillip had been a rabid atheist, and everything about him indicated that this position had been inherited. He'd described his mother as a bohemian occupying a shawl-draped house in Greenwich Village, the kind of mother he spoke to openly about girlfriends and drugs and sex. In the foremost pew, I saw the woman who must have been her, with papery white hands pressed in prayer and shoulders sunk in a posture of resignation. "Well, it's happened," her shoulders seemed to say.

Phillip had spoken of his mother often and with adulation. Of his father he'd said only that the man was a loser and he was dead. I'd pressed him for more. I'd liked that Phillip's father was dead; it made him more interesting. With this mote of information, I fashioned Phillip into someone I could pity and possibly save. I wound myself into a ball of his repressed suffering. I had been a very sensitive person then, my skin a tight membrane stretched thinly over gallons of fluid feeling. With just a light prod I could shape this feeling into expression. Most of the time I was too much of a coward to shape it around myself. Phillip, to my surprise, welcomed my displaced empathy. "Oh really?" he said, tantalized. He listened with interest as I described my vision of him. A boy terrified of becoming his father, whose greatest fear was dying young and nobody like the man who'd made him, whose depth of fear and grief were buried so deep they manifested as dismissal.

To my creation he'd added his mother:

"He wants to replace his dad—he wants to become the man worthy of dear Mommy's love! He fantasizes that *he* is what killed his dad."

"So overtly Freudian?" I had criticized. "Is his mother beautiful? Does he wish to sleep with her too?"

He considered my question seriously.

"Yeah, my mom's hot. Sure, I'd sleep with her, why not."

Phillip, it'd seemed, was totally unafraid. He'd do anything for extremities of experience that might be used for his art. "My art," he called it always, whereas I spoke of Art with a capital *A*, something I fancied belonged only to history, or to God, dead or not. Phillip would die young, I thought often; he would get himself killed. Often I worried he'd get me killed too.

The praying woman in the front pew turned back and stared accusingly. I clapped my hand over a gasp. She had Phillip's face almost exactly. It was drawn and hollow, fleshless, with eyes as round as coins. Were they looking at me?

I NEVER WANTED TO TAKE a photograph of Phillip. For weeks after we met I took no photographs at all. Intentionally, I'd left my camera packed in the suitcase pushed underneath my bed. Since I'd decided to "become a photographer" a year or so before, I'd carried a camera on my person wherever I went, and the motion of reaching for it had grown so reflexive that I felt naked when it wasn't there. This was the problem: I'd begun to use it as a shield. Whenever I found myself looking at something I didn't understand, I whipped out my camera and placed the lens between it and me.

The year before I met Phillip, I had taken a class with a famous professor. Standing before a photograph of my mother, flanked by students awaiting her judgment, she had spoken gently of my precision and technique, and of my natural formal eye. "Like the camera is an extension of her," quipped the professor's favorite, a broody Mark rumored to be the child of a respected sculptor. "No," he amended, "like she's a photographing machine." These words burrowed into me. In the photograph, which was black and white, my mother stood drying a bowl at the kitchen sink. The shape of my mother occupied the exact center of the kitchen window, a bright white rectangle lit by the setting sun, but this focal image was set off-center, perfect and askew. I looked away from the photograph, at window, wall, shadow, ceiling, and realized I was no longer capable of looking at something without seeing its potential for capture—imposing around it a frame. Where was my eye? I had come to the photograph with the simple but sincere desire to preserve my sight of beautiful fleeting things. Endlessly beautiful things, things I wanted to see forever, but which I'd have to give up: my mother would put down the dish, breaking her symmetry, would turn with irritation to me.

I kept the camera packed away. I challenged myself to really see what I was looking at before trying to fix it in image. Oh, I was uncomfortable all the time. In a foreign land, buried in first love, I heard constantly the whisper of "you must preserve this," which was really the cry of "you are afraid."

Finally Phillip was the one who unpacked the camera. "Well, well," he said, "what do we have here?" With wicked delight he climbed on top of the dresser, holding it beyond my reach. It was a small digital machine that I liked for its sweet spot of size and power; I could carry it and remain unseen. Phillip scrolled through the images stored on the memory card, and I watched his eyes nervously, searching for the realization that I was a better artist than he, better now *and* more promising.

"You've taken *no* photographs since we got here! Zero! Nil! Zip!"

Reluctantly I began to explain my reasoning. As I spoke my reluctance melted into eagerness. I drank his reactions thirstily— was he quizzical, intrigued, impressed?

"Well?" I said. "What do you think?"

He said nothing. He turned the dial to capture and hopped off the dresser. Head tilted, face screwed up in concentration, he aimed my camera at me. I protested, hiding. I was naked, as was he. He was aiming the camera at my untamed pubes, my pimply breasts. He pushed me onto the bed, pinning me down with his knees, stuck his fingers into me, and shot. Oh, he got hard. He pried me apart. He pressed the lens against my opening and shot into me—I protesting, shouting about ruining the equipment, about the dismal lighting—and then he put himself into me, and as he fucked me he shot and said, "Art, my little prude! This is fucking art!"

After I swore not to delete anything, he returned the camera to me. I clicked through the shots. Phillip's breath was hot on my shoulder; idly his hand tickled my clit. The hard flash, the chaotic framing, the grotesque focus: it was pornography. Did Phillip see this? The latter shots were not just ugly but indecipherable, blurs of flesh obscured by the gloss of my slime. "I feel ill," I said, truthfully, and he said, "It's how I see you."

He propped himself up on his elbows and grinned at me.

"I don't know if it's true but I really want to say it," he said. "I love you. I love you!"

For a moment, I let myself be stunned.

"Okay," I finally said.

I made an ugly laugh: "I certainly don't love you."

But I was lying, it turned out, lying to squash the sick excitement kicking into realization inside me. Like any good American girl, I had dreamed of this moment—the blond-haired, blue-eyed boy, the exchange of fluids and words—as the beginning of my real life.

PHILLIP WENT ON A TRIP to the eastern side of the island with the other Americans, as part of his Americans-in-a-foreign-land class. I'd laughed at him until the moment he stepped out the door. "Have fun on your field trip," I said. "Don't forget your permission slip!" I'd been looking forward to getting some space, to the emptiness of the house, and to walking the streets of the city alone. That is, without Phillip. Phillip prodding me constantly to interpret and to dispute, to make him see things the way I thought they ought to be seen. As Phillip piled into a van with the gaggle of fair Americans, I imagined the sun, the ocean, the high limestone walls of the university, smiling broadly and beckoning to me.

But when the door closed and the van drove away, I was hollow. Hollow and agitated, I looked out the window at the oppressive sun and had a headache. For days I was like this, my misery made worse only by refusing to allow that Phillip was the cause of it. I filled my days with exciting things that excited me because I could imagine telling Phillip: I imagined his eyes gleaming with envy. Misery made me brave. That week, I marched up to the art professor after class and asked if there was such a thing here as "office hours." He laughed and said, "What is an office?" but sure, the hours here were plenty. We met at the professors' lounge and had coffee on the balcony. Coffees were very small and sweet in this country, and we sipped ours slowly.

The professor talked theatrically, with exaggerated facial expressions and gestures, waving his hands even more than he did in class. Though I did not understand much of what he said, I believed him a brilliant man. I tried to converse with him; I felt it would be a wasted opportunity if I said nothing. "What do you think drives art?" I said. "Is it emotion and expression, or a desire to capture reality?"

"Desire?" He seized on the word and spoke rapidly and incomprehensibly, for ten or fifteen minutes straight. Finally I picked out a few words I understood: "the hours" were leaving us today, but we would meet again tomorrow to discuss "desire and reality."

The next day I arrived to find a man sitting beside him on the balcony, a student, perhaps, from another class. Thinking I had misunderstood, I turned to leave, but the professor shouted, "Hey, China!" and waved me over.

"This is Picasso," he said when I sat down.

I nearly spat out my coffee.

"I'm an artist," the boy named Picasso said, smiling slantly, "a painter."

For the remaining days that Phillip was gone, I saw this Picasso. He took me to galleries around the city, galleries hidden in narrow alleys and dark living rooms, in abandoned mansions and underground bars. He introduced me to artists and musicians and writers, invited me to open-air concerts where we danced with his friends in the warm night breeze. I was moved by the art, by the music, by the company. Everything, I exclaimed over melting strawberry and chocolate ice creams, was top-notch. Picasso explained that despite the general poverty, there was superb funding of the arts—an artist received the same monthly subsidy as a doctor or a professor or a bus driver, and besides, everyone in this country was bored to death so had plenty of time to read and ruminate and appreciate life's higher pleasures. "It's true," his friend Michele chimed in. Michele was the son of a diplomat, a rare person who had traveled and even lived outside of the country. "I was shocked by the poverty in Buenos Aires, shocked!" Michele said. "People sleeping on the streets!" He punched the air with his finger. "Our houses might be small and crumbling, but at least they're *all* small and crumbling."

Picasso was a gentleman. Unlike other men in this country, he respected my physical boundaries, and seemed to understand that despite my easy assimilation, my American body still possessed a solid notion of privacy. When we greeted and parted he kissed me chastely on the cheek, with a light hand on my arm. He walked me home every night, though I had never felt unsafe walking alone. He did not come to the door but waited at the gate until I was inside. He was very handsome, with the finely balanced yet seductive features of mixed-race beauty, so handsome that I was often flattened with amazement when I looked at him. Every night we walked home together, I fantasized that Phillip had returned early and was waiting anxiously for me on the porch; I fantasized his burning look of jealousy when he saw Picasso and me.

PHILLIP'S CLASS RETURNED IN THE morning. The house, humid and still, chattered and clunked suddenly with English and the careless energy of the Americans. I'd had visions of being occupied when this moment came, off on some wonderful adventure—at the very least I was determined to be aloof. But excitement bubbled up in me, helpless and pure. I threw open my door and went out shouting Phillip's name guilelessly. Happy like a girl, I saw him, walking through the front gate, and was stopped in my tracks, my body responding instantly while my mind slowly perceived. He wore a ragged tank top and a crooked, guilty smile. Scattered over his neck and chest were red-brown marks—"Are you hurt?" my mouth asked dully even as recognition arrived—on his thin white skin, the crescents of mouths, of teeth, the unmistakable marks of love.

Later, he would describe the encounter painstakingly, and I would listen painstakingly too, with a rigid, rigorous dispassion, as if swallowing a bitter medicine I was convinced would cleanse me of something worse. He watched me with detached curiosity, observing, documenting. Was it possible he was following my lead? He told of how he had ventured out alone with his poor language skills, missing me at first, wishing I were there to guide him, and wandered around aimlessly until he found himself drinking with "some local guys." High-spirited, friendly, the local guys warmed him up, sharing their rum, and when they ran out Phillip purchased two bottles more and sat with them on the seawall, passing the drink around, pouring straight from the necks of the bottles into their throats. All this time the guys were asking him questions, throwing out simple words like "girls" and "love," and when the bottles were nearly empty Phillip found that he could suddenly understand them, with magical clarity: "You want some love?" they were asking. "You want some good love?"

"Come on, I couldn't pass it up," Phillip said. "I wasn't going to come all this way just to hunker down with a Chinese girlfriend! Besides, you're barely Chinese!"

The local guys took him to two local girls, one big and one thin. He chose the big girl because he considered her more authentic.

With clinical precision, he described what the girl did to him, how she'd bitten his neck, his arm, his chest, his ass, and took him into her, the things he tried to say and the things she said that he did not understand. In the end, he said, it was more or less the same. So much for "good love"; when it came to sex, women everywhere were the same. This he proclaimed as the revelatory result of years of dedicated research.

Oh, I suffered. Never had my mind been so certain of one thing—that I should run from this vileness, run now before its rot infected me—while another part of me ached unremittingly for its opposite. Was it my heart? I hope not. I threw myself into the streets, thoughts and emotions roiling, roiling so turbulently not a single one could form fully before another rose to smother it with equal force and urgency. On the streets I received the expected male attention, which, baffling as it had been when I first arrived—baffling because, having never received male attention before, I knew myself to be ugly, sexless at best—now soothed me. "Marry me, Chinagirl!" men shouted from the opposite end of the street, or "The most beautiful China in the world!" Though I knew these praises were sung to everybody, that even timid men whispered compliments to a passing woman as if out of obligation, the words emboldened me. "Perhaps I *am* beautiful," I thought, "I *am* wanted, I *am* desired, Phillip is *damn lucky!*"

I went to Picasso. I continued as I had when Phillip was gone, drinking and partying with my own locals, praising myself for how differently I acted from Phillip; I was not just seeking novelty but making friends, friends who liked my company even when I was not buying their liquor, who liked to talk passionately with me about Art and Politics and Society. I imagined we would keep in touch. I imagined Picasso was falling in love with me. Did I want him? I don't know. Even now I don't know. In my fantasies, the clock stopped when he leaned in to kiss me; I replayed the moment again and again with different gestures and words, deliberating how I might respond—if I would push him away or take him eagerly, if I would blink back tears or laugh in celebration—luxuriating in that delicious moment in which I possessed the power to hurt Phillip, and would choose whether to use it or not.

To my great impatience Picasso did not try to kiss me. He did pay me special attention, acting at turns like a guide and a guard, and wouldn't let any other men near me. I thought I saw an inner struggle inside him, a deliberation about whether and how to make a move. What was stopping him? The knowledge that I would be leaving in a matter of months? The desire to differentiate himself from the aggressive masculinity of his peers? A heightened class consciousness? Impatient, emboldened by drink, I made the first move. "I want to see your paintings," I said.

Picasso paused—"Oh?" He made a show of false modesty before relenting. "Tomorrow," he said affectionately.

TOMORROW I LEFT THE HOUSE. I told no one where I was going. Through the heat I moved languorously but resolutely, to indicate to whoever might be watching that I was headed in the direction of significance and unbothered about it. I met Picasso on the university steps, and we walked east, toward the old town, Picasso answering my inquiries about his work courteously, with extra caution it seemed: shy. We stopped before a tall building with peeling jay-blue paint. Double doors opened into a dark lobby that smelled of urine and antiseptic. "The elevator, alas," Picasso said, "it's always broken." I laughed in sympathy and followed him up the stairs to the eleventh floor. The stairwell echoed faintly with laughter and music, and smelled of onions frying. Students squeezed past us with casual pardons, some turning to take a second look at me. This was a dormitory, I learned, for students from the provinces, a piece of shit but at least it was free. He hadn't invited me earlier, Picasso admitted, for shame of its shabbiness.

"What? This isn't so shabby," I said. Picasso raised an eyebrow at me.

I thought I saw in him then something I recognized. How foolish that I hadn't seen it before, that I hadn't even thought to ask. Of course: for all of Michele's talk of economic equality, his vision was also a dream. I thought of Picasso's deference to Michele, the son of the diplomat, light-skinned easygoing Michele who in a different climate could have passed for European, like so many of the students at the university. I thought of how Picasso almost always wore the same neatly pressed red polo, and his general hesitation and politeness, his considered caution, his careful observation. Suddenly the person before me was illuminated with a clarity of vision that touched me. "I'm fine! How wonderful! They're beautiful!" I said too effusively when I finally stepped inside his room, drenched in sweat and breathless while he looked as he always did, like he had just bathed and coifed his hair. He shared the room with five others, who were all out but for a studious engineer who sat on his bed reading and was not surprised or interested to see me. Picasso's painting studio was a corner between his bunk and the window, one mini salon wall of small canvases, a stool, and an easel made from a clipboard and a broken chair. He had asked me to come at this hour because the light was best at this time of day.

He painted—like his namesake. Cubist portraits—mostly of women, white women, by the look of the hair—but with bright, nearly scorching colors. Colors that matched the heat, I said, that evoked it, almost as a sense memory. Collections of lopped-off body parts—a boob here, an eye there—the portraits were nonetheless composed; there was an appreciation in the artist's eye for the beauty of the female form. I told him this.

"You're too generous."

Then, cautiously: "Do you want me to paint you?

"I could paint you, if you wanted," he repeated. "A Picasso, just for you."

"Oh!" Surprised, I was quickly seduced: my very own Picasso! How romantic these words sounded in his mouth, romantic and arch. It occurred to me that I might repay him, in a way, for his friendship, that I might share some of my relative wealth with my friend, and without revealing my hand—even that I might dignify him by paying him for his art. "Yes, how special! I'll commission a portrait from you."

Picasso smiled. He gestured for me to step onto a small balcony. There the light was "sublime" and we could have some privacy. He positioned me beside a halved soda can stuffed with cigarette butts, leaning against the railing. He moved with the practiced confidence of one who knew exactly what he was doing. I, on the other hand, had never sat for a portrait before and must have looked very stiff. I tried to stay still. "Don't worry about it," Picasso said. "Be natural, change your face, move your body, whatever you like. Painting is dynamic, not like photography, freezing a moment in time"—he winked at me—"but a medium to capture the subject moving through time, caught in its loco-motion."

We talked, he painted, slowly the sun set, and the light was exquisite, as he'd promised, the pale pulsing blue of the hot sky, the yellow haze evaporating from the horizon, the blazing white where they met: charged. When he finished he set the painting aside and scooted next to me.

"Let me see it," I said.

"Let it dry."

"I've never been looked at so intensely."

"Did you like it?"

"I don't know."

He took my face into his hand. "I've painted Americans before," he said, "but you're my first Chinese girl." His mouth hung slightly open, his eyelids at half-mast. "You know, sometimes after I paint for a customer, they want more."

He kissed me.

Time barreled ahead, not waiting as in my fantasy. My mind lingered as it had been trained. It stopped at the kiss and replayed it, slowed it, replayed the words, picking the sentence apart. Then the body called, and my mind raced after, frantic, barely registering sensation—sensation overwhelmed every faculty. The breeze: we were out in the open, somebody might see us, his engineer roommate or a person on the street; his sighs, loud: they might hear him; then skin, the setting sun scorching the face, the dirt beneath the thighs, cutting into the flesh, so even as he pushed himself inside, I did not realize it, perceiving only coarseness, the usual pain, thinking that I should check the expiration on the condom wrapper if I could find it. His terribly handsome face, wearing an expression so intense it looked like a mask of pleasure he had pulled on, bobbed above me. I squinted and tried to see it, voicing his name, Picasso, as if to remind myself who this was, that this face and body belonged not to an animated statue but to a person I knew—and what did I know of him? My mind slammed into the present and spotted us, understanding finally that we were fucking.

"We are known to be good lovers," he said softly, sucking a breast, and he was right, I came violently as I pushed him off of me.

He walked me home as he always did. At the gate he produced the small square canvas on which he'd painted me. "Oh," I said, blinking. "I'll—the money's inside." I went and got my cash. "How much?" I said. I handed it over without counting. I forgave Phillip. I went back to him. I didn't see Picasso again.

MY LOVER WAS A GOOD man. He loved and celebrated easily, qualities that endeared him to me. "Such a good guy," he would exclaim about anybody, and fervently when drunk: "Truly a good guy!"

I wondered whether, if my lover had met Phillip, they would have gotten along. If Phillip would have been deemed, in boozy goodwill, "a good guy." No, I decided triumphantly. My lover would have been puzzled by Phillip, puzzled because he had never cultivated an ability to pin down his dislike. "What a weirdo," I might say to goad my lover, and he would laugh good-naturedly and agree: "Yes, he really was weird!"

How this lover had changed me. Once, I had found honor in naked honesty: if there was a wound, I pressed it. I'd taken pride in dredging up buried pain; pain was how I recognized another. With previous lovers, I'd eaten up stories of other women hungrily, hurting myself with jealousy until it felt like love. I had tried it with this one too. He'd been married before me, after all.

"Do you really want to know?" he'd asked.

"Don't you?"

"Not really."

I saw he was telling the truth. I saw he had no desire to hurt me, or to be hurt. His instinct to look away: it was trust. Perhaps it was a little cowardly. But once I learned to follow this instinct, to rely on it, deploying it with even greater skill than he, I was happier.

I decided not to tell my lover about Phillip, who was irrelevant to our happiness. Just as I'd never told Phillip about Picasso, I realized suddenly. I'd told no one about Picasso. I'd not looked at the portrait and could not say what had happened to it. I was remembering it and him now for the first time.

Of Phillip: I'd opened my mouth to speak of the news of death, and closed it. Quite literally I swallowed my words.

"What?" my lover said. "Tell me."

I kept my mouth shut. Transparently I changed the subject by pouring us drinks. I seduced my lover, kissing his neck and chin, pressing vodka onto his tongue. He swatted at me—"I see what you're doing, tell me!" Finally I said, "It's nothing, just—"

My lover folded his arms.

"Oh, just that I'm not a very good person!"

"Oh?" he said, laughing. He was always laughing at me.

"Yes. I'm too interested in my own survival."

He cocked an eyebrow: "*Oh*."

"And I have no good reason for wanting to survive—"

He wanted to laugh harder but waited for me to finish.

"—except that I like being alive."

Oh, he laughed. He tackled me, folding me at the waist. The conversation was over: now we could make love. We clinked our glasses. I let him fall over me. I closed my eyes and sank into it. I felt that I was good, very good. I loved being alive.

I THOUGHT I SHOULD PAY my condolences. After the service, I joined the line of people waiting to speak with the woman who wore Phillip's aged face. "Who are you?" she said when I got to the front. "One of Phillip's girlfriends?" She made a noise that sounded like a scoff, like Phillip's scoff, like she was bored to death.

She was wearing black, of course. On her black-shawled shoulders little flakes of dandruff sat sprinkled like confetti.

I had the urge to say, "I mostly paint, I'm a painter!"

Or,

"Sorry for your loss," as I was supposed to.

Or,

"Don't you know who I am?"

Well, I wasn't that famous. But I had become an artist after all, unlike Phillip, who had only managed to die. My modest success, I suspected, was the reason I'd been invited. Behind Phillip's mother, the woman who'd emailed me milled about in a group of aging hipsters, trying to catch my eye. Vaguely I knew of her as the owner of a new gallery that had opened in the gentrified blocks of Chinatown, a tiny concrete box on whose walls, as far as I knew, had not yet hung a Chinese American work. I had not known she knew Phillip. But in the eulogy she'd spoken with intimacy, describing his noncareer as if it were part of some underground scene.

I heard myself:

"I don't feel sorry for you.

"That's right," I was saying, to Phillip's mother and anyone else, "my well of empathy has gone dry. I'm sure as hell not reaching in there for Phillip."

DID PHILLIP WANT TO LIVE? Did he love life, as I did? My imagination ended at the question. The image of Phillip's death had been fixed in me long before it came true. Perhaps I still possessed it, somewhere, in a dark storage container where I'd thrown the camera upon returning to America those many years ago, the memory card rusting in its metal cage.

Before we left the island, Phillip and I had taken a number of excursions together to "gather material." Noticing that I still kept the camera stashed, thinking I was stuck, or perhaps that love had overtaken my ambition and artistry, Phillip claimed that he'd conceived of these excursions for me. On one of them, we'd wandered into an old cemetery at the outskirts of the city whose iron gates had once been locked by a chain that now lay in pieces in the grass. The grounds were overgrown. Dried weeds sprouted from the cracks of grand crumbling tombstones and crunched beneath our feet. We walked into a circle of crypts guarded by faceless seraphs and saints, garish displays of wealth and piety, the false idols of the previous social order.

Phillip was delighted. Death, after all, was his proclaimed subject. He skipped through the graves giddily, launching himself off slabs of limestone, climbing up half the side of a marble crypt before slipping and sliding down, cracking the stillness with his laughs. "Are you getting all this?" he shouted at me.

"Yup, yup," I replied reflexively as the camera hung limp at my hip, wondering: Was Phillip putting on a show for *me*? I walked with my head down, following the edge of my questioning. When I looked up I was standing in a field of holes. Gone were the monuments, the seraphs, the shade of untrimmed trees. These graves lay open and waiting. Some of their lids had been pried off and thrown to one side; some had been smashed in and lay in a heap at the bottom of the rectangular cavity. I peered into one, unthinking. Not until after my mouth let out a gasp did my eyes name what they were seeing: bone, skull, body.

I felt hands on my back. They pushed. I fell hard. I turned and faced a blinding sun. A figure moved over it, casting me into shadow. He was holding my camera, must have stolen it off me. He straddled the grave and shot.

"What if you let me kill you?" he said.

He hopped down. He put a hand around my throat. I don't know if he continued to shoot. My ears were full of his voice, narrating. How he felt: super strong, he said, like I'm having a great fuck. How my skin felt under his: soft, like putty, he said, sticky with sweat. Pretty gross, he said with a laugh, describing my face: my eyes, bulging; my mouth, open, drooling. You don't look pretty, he said, but I'm getting hard. Say what you're thinking, he said.

Then it was over. I was standing and Phillip was lying down. I was holding the camera; he had shoved it into my hands. "Now you do me," he said. "Come on!"

For the rest of our time together, I would point the lens randomly, shooting without looking, without attempting focus or form, to prevent this urging voice—"Come on!"—from resurfacing. I already knew that whatever I took from here would have to be unplaceable, that I had neither desire nor ability to preserve any fragment of my experience to represent a "culture" or "society" or "moment in time." Perhaps I already knew that I would never look at these photographs, and would never voluntarily pick up a camera again.

The sun sank before us as we left the cemetery. I was deep inside myself, still and calm. I breathed in the hot dusk air. I saw I was not bleeding. The bruises would appear later, deep pools of blue and gray emerging beneath my scraped flesh like an alien skin. A true skin, it had felt then, and I wore it proudly.

Beside me, Phillip twirled a femur he'd taken from the grave.

"What if you *had* killed me?" I looked at him with curiosity. "What if I had died?"

"I guess I'd go to jail? That would suck."

He grinned.

"Come on, I was fully consumed in the present, I was fully spontaneous, fully alive!"

He was. Joyful, exuberant, like a clever child discovering and testing his abilities. He pulled me to him and kissed me. "Don't you think one moment of pure freedom is worth more than some arbitrary ideas of good and evil?" he said. I blinked back at him, examining the lines on his brow, the three bumps of his nose, the sunken curve of his cheek. If I looked for it, in the dancing blue of his sight, I could find the outline of my own face. "Oh, I'd be so sad if you died," he was saying. "I'd be heartbroken! Yeah, I'd miss you! But I'd come out of it a better artist, wouldn't I, my art would be so profound!

"Wouldn't it be worth it," he said in all seriousness, "to die for great art?"

At that moment I must have seen, though my vision would not clear for many, many years, how harmless I appeared. Phillip had posed for me in the grave, exposing his soft neck, oh yes: he had invited me to kill him. Yet it would never occur to him, not really, that I actually could—that I might become the artist, and he the corpse.

Suffering

Ling is suffering, her husband is dead so suffering is the story of her life. Then her suffering begins to appear as patches on her skin—raw, white, like gashes in flesh before the blood floods in. Appearing first in inconspicuous places, they grow and spread: from hairline to cheek, from cheek to chin, from behind the ear to the corner of one watching eye. They grow and form in shapes cragged and unpredictable, so unpredictable they seem alive.

Ling washes her face. She lotions her face, liberally. Her face shines oily and slick. She hides from the sun, opening an umbrella whenever she steps outdoors. Still the patches persist. She is a country girl, a peasant born, her skin dull and yellow, "dirt-like," so many have said. Now the patches, creeping out and in, expose an underlayer, naked and peeled.

"Her suffering begins to appear"—Ling would not put it this way. For Ling, suffering is a tool, wielded by the human and the divine. The abstract manifests as concrete, the intangible as felt. Suffering can be hard like a slap or it can fester, like grit beneath the nail. Feeling hardens into form, allegory into event. Ling doesn't need pigmentation to describe her grief. Her suffering has always been material.

No, when I ask for her version of events, she says, "I met a man. He wants to marry me. Now someone is poisoning my facial cream."

The first of many poisons to enter Ling's life.

The cream is a good brand, Western, the same one Little Sister uses, Little Sister who lives in America. In the department stores on Nanjing Lu, a palm-sized tub sells for a year of Ling's rent. She has used the cream sparingly, one finger's smear a day; in two months it recedes a mere centimeter from the rim. It is a gift, of course, a gift from Little Sister. Ling does not typically accept gifts, and especially not from Little Sister. She took this one only because of the appearance of the man, the man she calls Mr. Fu.

MR. FU IS OLD AND UGLY. Twenty-five years her senior, with gray hair and liver spots, unabashedly sporting a cane. In the picture he sends he does not smile, but between the lips Ling spies a sliver of yellow teeth. Are they dentures? She imagines the slippery tongue behind them, sour and thin.

Mr. Fu has distinguished himself, in his Baidu personal listing, with sincerity and straightforwardness. In his correspondence there are no exaggerated promises or gross overtures, no lines of poetry or false compliments. He summarizes his personal details—age, income, housing—and expresses his desire to meet a good, honest woman with whom he might have a child. In Ling's calculation they are a good match: she with relative youth and fertility, he with a pension and promise of stability. In their exchange of messages, she learns that he is once divorced and has no children, the separation his ex-wife's choice. She in turn informs him of her first marriage, and of her son, who is ten. She is willing and able to have another child, she writes to him, and by law, as a widow, she can.

In their exchanges Ling refers to this other child as a son, and she knows this pleases Mr. Fu.

Mr. Fu always responds with respectful practicality. When he sends the unflattering portrait, Ling is further assured. Here is a man, at last, presenting himself exactly as he is.

They agree to meet.

"I KNOW HOW IMPORTANT A pretty face is for a man," Ling tells me, adding, "For any kind of man."

So she makes herself pretty. She buys new clothes, she cuts her hair. In the middle of all this, Little Sister lands in Shanghai. Little Sister, a banker in America, comes home a few times a year for work and tears through the family like a storm. In her wake, pains and wants long buried fly about like loose foliage. Little Sister demands that the family comes where and when suits her, and the family scrambles to meet the demands. Behaving, Ling thinks, like servants. At the hotel where Little Sister is staying, at six, they'll all have dinner. Ling isn't going.

Where's your sentiment? Little Sister says, a ringing voice in her phone. Have you no heart? Think of Hai, how refreshing for him to get out of the house. Ma even took the train, it's a rare opportunity.

Ling hangs up.

The night of the dinner, at nine o'clock, the buzzer rings. Hai is in bed, Ling in her pajamas. Little Sister is already coming up the stairs, plastic bags in both hands. Leftovers, she says, pushing through the door. She sets the bags on the table. They smell like garlic. Behind her, Brother lugs a suitcase onto the landing. Behind Brother and the suitcase is Brother's Wife, wearing a purple suit and a stupid little smile. Brother's Wife looks stupid in order to look harmless. This, thinks Ling, is the first of that woman's many despicable traits.

Ling shuts the door behind them, glaring.

Ma was tired, Little Sister says, she's sleeping at the hotel. I booked an extra room with two beds. You and Hai should come enjoy for a few nights!

Hai has to go to school, Ling says.

Little Sister is always talking like this, like her garlicky leftovers and hotel beds where strangers have fucked the night before are made of solid gold. She opens the suitcase and pulls out clothes, talking as she goes: They're great quality, American, good brands, Macy's, Ann Taylor, very expensive, all in great condition! Lao Wang wanted me to throw them out, but I thought, what a waste, just because I don't want them doesn't mean someone else might not. As they say, one man's trash is another's treasure . . .

Her tone changes. Perhaps she hears herself. Now she speaks with eagerness, holding up a sequined magenta blouse: Wow, Ling, this color is so flattering on you! Whatever you don't want, you can just throw away.

Brother's Wife fishes out a flowery ball of yellow yarn. What a beautiful scarf, she says. How generous of Sister to offer such nice things!

Ling wants nothing. She doesn't dress like Little Sister, with her bright reds and pinks, her shoulder pads and gold buttons. She rolls the zipped suitcase into the bedroom where she and her husband once slept, now a storage room stacked full of trunks and furniture from Little Sister's demolished Shanghai apartment. Near the front sits an old computer from that apartment, which Brother hooked up to the internet, the singular item of use: Hai needs the computer for homework, and she to message Mr. Fu. Ling closes the door and looks at Little Sister. She says, Are you finally going to do something about all this trash?

Oh, I almost forgot, Little Sister says, syrupy and apologetic. She digs in her purse and retrieves the facial cream. It's the same one I use, very expensive. Sixty American dollars a tub!

Brother's Wife eyes the tub. Ling takes it with cautious curiosity, thinking of Mr. Fu.

Little Sister produces a small bag of cosmetics of the same brand and hands it to Brother's Wife. It is clearly less valuable, a free gift people like Ling's sister get for buying many things. Brother's Wife gushes with gratitude.

"She kept the scarf too," Ling tells me, adding, "It was the color of a newborn's poop."

IN THE MONTHS LEADING UP to her first meeting with Mr. Fu, Ling applies the facial cream. It smells like rose and something she can't quite name. "Maybe it was wealth." Does her skin improve? Like magic. Pink glows under the film of her cheeks, a new face being born. She runs her fingers over her skin and finds it taut but not too tight.

They meet at a restaurant near the metro station for lunch. Though they are just two, Mr. Fu has booked a private room. She recognizes him instantly: gray hair, long face, small and crinkled eyes. He is taller than expected, small from a distance but when he stands to greet her, she cranes her neck to smile. Her husband was tall too—not just tall but wide, a giant.

I've ordered, he says. He motions at the waitress to pull out the chair beside him. Ling sits.

So here you are, Ling'er.

She likes the sound of his voice. Her name in his mouth, with the diminutive *'er*, sounds like the name of a fairy, a creature he might carry in his pocket wherever he pleases. She reads his face and finds no deception. Just a few lines of weariness around the mouth, to be expected from a man his age. He watches her attentively. He turns the table's glass top, and the waiting cold dishes appear before her one by one. Sugared cucumber, sliced lamb, chopped malantou with aged tofu.

The waitresses begin to serve. The glass top spins, hot dishes arrive, Ling spoons into her bowl and eats. The air is fragrant with steam. Mr. Fu has ordered enough for all ten places set around the table. Afterward, the meal will look barely eaten, and like people who understand how to sit with wealth, they will leave without a second glance. Mr. Fu's tastes are sweet, the tastes of old Shanghai: tang cu spareribs, stewed lotus root stuffed with sticky rice, lion's head meatball in sweet soy gravy, white shrimp like crystal candy. They are flavors Ling knows well from her years in the city, though they've never entered her own cravings. Sugar is a city flavor, Ling thinks: refined. Her own tastes are for the salty and sour, the smack of preserving brine.

Mr. Fu watches her eat and talks, filling in the details of his life. He is newly retired, on a government pension; he worked mostly in the urban planning department for Hongko. At the height of his career he was the assistant to the district chief, the third-most-powerful man in the district. He attributes his success in career to his failure in love, or vice versa; with such things it is hard to tell. Ling listens. A palette of browns stains her bowl, a record of each cloying sauce. In contrast, Mr. Fu's bowl shines, perfectly untouched, except for one glistening bone.

Did you ever think of remarrying before now? Ling asks.

Mr. Fu picks up a sparerib and pops it into his mouth. In a moment a second bone appears, taking its place beside the first.

Of course, he says.

He reaches for another piece of meat.

OUTSIDE THE RESTAURANT, HE HAILS a cab—for himself, Ling thinks, until he pulls the handle and stands waiting, holding the door open for her. Oh, she is about to say, I planned to walk, but he has already folded a hundred-yuan bill into her hand. She is stepping into the back seat, turning for a last goodbye, when he says:

You never said how your husband passed away.

She is unprepared. It has not occurred to her how she might answer this question to Mr. Fu: the most obvious oversight in the world. Hasn't she herself asked Mr. Fu the details of his first marriage as if it were her right to know?

She says, In a workplace accident.

It is what they told the mourners.

Mr. Fu says, I see.

The door shuts, the taxi is off. Ling turns to look out the back window. Mr. Fu gets into a black car. How small he looks, she thinks, with his bent back and silver cane, receding into smaller smallness as her cab drives away. She feels a tenderness she cannot explain. In her apartment she stands for many minutes, dazed, picking things up and putting them down, resting her hands on the windowsill, on the television, on her own face. She looks at her hands, at her reflection in the windowpane. How odd, she has the feeling that small bits at her edges have detached themselves and are floating softly away. In the courtyard below, children are coming home. She watches the black dots of their heads, dispersing, and in a flash remembers why she'd planned to walk from lunch. Her child, her Hai—she'd meant to pick him up from school.

Outside the closed school gates, Hai sits with another boy. The other boy is bigger, with a square head; together they crouch at the curb playing with a toy truck. Hai looks up, his face contrite in surprise. But Ling does not scold him for fraternizing with strangers. Disoriented, still perhaps "in the fog of love," Ling smiles at the other boy and asks his name. Hu, the boy replies.

And you are in Hai's class?

No, Hai-mama, but we're the same year.

You're big for your age.

That's what everyone says.

Is someone coming to get you?

No, Hai-mama, my mother lets me walk alone.

Can he come with us? Hai looks hopefully at Ling, adding quickly, He lives in the building next door.

They walk home, Hai with a spring in his step. Ling lets the boys run ahead, holding their hands only when crossing the street. The sky shines clear, and the afternoon sun sparkles through magnolia leaves. The clarity, the light: a revelation. So this is why she was made late, for this vision of two sons.

THAT NIGHT, THE FIRST PATCH appears. Ling sees it as she washes her face, and, assuming it a spot of soap, wipes it with her towel. It doesn't wipe off. She leans into the mirror and picks it with her nail. She runs her finger over the white spot and finds it continuous with her skin.

When did it appear? Was it present in the morning, through her lunch with Mr. Fu? She wipes it again, hard. Her skin turns angry and red. She gives up. She applies a dab of facial cream, though she already applied it in the morning. She hopes the spot will be gone when she wakes.

By morning it has grown.

She washes her face. She picks up the tub of cream and dips her finger in. She feels—a sting. A venomous gold flashes behind her lids, the memory of Brother's Wife's face: her envy when Little Sister hands Ling the expensive prize. Brother is a good man, good and simple, born after the famine and two miscarriages; with him Mother learned love. He is the only person in the family

Ling can talk to without the urge to scream. But he married a viper, a greedy woman whose greed runs green in her blood. The women in that family are known to go after men belonging to other women, chasing fortune, dispensing illness and tragedy to whoever stands in their way. Brother's Wife is no different. She will do anything for Little Sister's money.

Little Sister's money. This is the root of Ling's problems. Everybody wants a piece, everybody except Ling. Her refusals are of no use. Everybody—and Brother's Wife foremost—assumes Ling is swimming in it: How else is she, husbandless and jobless, without even a primary-school degree, raising a healthy, intelligent son alone in China's most expensive city? Little Sister, stupid, proud, trusting, makes a show of offering Ling money at every public opportunity. Since her husband's death, Ling has placed each red envelope of Little Sister's goodwill in a drawer she will never touch.

She shows me a smear of white cream. I suggest she test it behind the ear, as for an allergy. "Allergy?" She laughs. Still, she pulls back her hair and smudges the cream there. Then Hai is at the door of the bathroom, wiping his sleepy eyes.

This is Tuesday. By Friday the stains have migrated over her neck and face. "The results of the poison test"—she pauses for dramatic effect—"are very positive." She no longer uses the cream, but it is too late: she looks like a reverse milk cow. That is what Hu says, one evening when she goes down to fetch Hai. Children can be cruel, but perhaps there is kindness in Hu's candor, a warning like a slap. When Hu's mother comes down to bring him in, Ling glimpses in the folds of the woman's coat the edges of a yellow scarf. The same poop yellow of the scarf Brother's Wife took from Little Sister's suitcase of trash.

So this is how Brother's Wife has managed it, planting spies in Ling's neighborhood. Ling opens her eyes and sees: the watching looks, the passing whispers, the neighbors who stand in their doorways and stare. In the mornings she sees dust blown in beneath the slat of the front door, and minuscule rips in the mosquito netting stretched across their windows. She installs new locks on her doors and windows. She rolls a towel in the crease of the door and jams the knob with a chair. She logs in to Baidu to postpone her next meeting with Mr. Fu. She writes that she is ill.

THE FOLLOWING MONDAY SHE GOES to the bank and withdraws five hundred yuan. It is an account her husband left, her husband who abandoned them, yes, but who was after all not a bad man. Along with his savings, he left her ownership of a shikumen room in Jing'an, which she rents out for a thousand yuan a month. For such a prime location she can earn much more, but she doesn't have the heart to evict her tenant, an old migrant from Xinjiang who collects used bottles and cans. As a principle, Ling refuses to soften her suffering by transferring it to others. She knows she will one day be rewarded for her endurance. The knowledge is instinctual, animal, like the knowledge of a sense: flowers smell sweet, rot smells foul.

On Wednesday, Hai will stay late at school to prepare for an upcoming exam. Ling has followed the path I've suggested, procuring the name of a doctor with good ratings on Baidu. She will take the extra hours to go to the hospital, where this doctor will heal her skin. She will bring the cream and the doctor will examine it to discover what kind of poison was used.

It isn't just vanity, Ling tells me. Her beauty is an investment in Mr. Fu, and Mr. Fu is an investment in her future, in Hai's.

What actually happens is this:

On Tuesday night, after dinner, which consists of simple, healthy dishes—tomato and egg, cabbage, and ox bone soup—Hai grows pale and irritated. He puts his homework away, complaining of nausea. His forehead is hot, his skin is white, his lips flaming red. He vomits when he tries to stand. He vomits again, and in the bile she sees flecks of red, some brownish, some bright, flecks of what could only be blood. She cleans the floor and puts Hai in the tub. After the bath she gives him a bowl of hot water with ginger and puts him to bed. That night he sleeps fitfully, forehead burning, calling out for his father.

Ling takes Hai to the hospital with the five hundred yuan. At the hospital gate he vomits again, this time nothing but bile. For three days he stays in the hospital, throwing up everything he eats. At night he convulses in his sleep. He is already a skinny boy, with a big head and a little body. Ling returns to the bank to withdraw more money. She takes the bus to the temple with the golden roof where her husband's ashes are kept. She buys big bundles of the biggest incense and burns the sticks before every pusa in the dian. Before the statue of Guanyin she knocks her head to the ground nine times. She purchases a five-hundred-yuan blessing in Hai's name.

Finally Hai keeps down a meal of solid food. They leave the hospital with a bag of pills. She returns to the bank, withdrawing more money to pay the fees.

What was put in the food to sicken Hai? And who? Who is so heartless she'll poison a child in order to torture his mother? Brother's Wife is vindictive, she poisoned the cream, of this Ling is nearly sure. But does she have the guts to touch her own nephew? No, this is something else. Ling is missing something—she considers the possibilities she's overlooked, and is frozen by the feeling of gears moving, pieces falling into place. The signs she missed, the signs she misread. She has been misdirected by the yellow scarf, which could be anyone's. How foolish to think Brother's Wife would bribe a neighbor with a gift she knows Ling has seen. The gathering observations in Ling's memory are ordering, clicking into meaning: At the temple the day before, there was a man. The man wore a brown coat with a checkered pattern, and prayed behind her, visiting the same deities as she, following her even into the room where she stood before her dead husband's name on a plaque. On the bus to the hospital, she saw him too, noting the pattern on his coat. The more she remembers, the more details come: the diagonal checkering on the coat, a unique pattern; the spot on the bus where the man stood, despite a nearby empty seat. He pulled a mobile phone from his pocket and clicked a message, stashing it in his pocket just as she turned to look. It is possible he was at the bank too. Now everything starts to make sense. Brother's Wife has nothing to do with Hai's ailments; no, they have to do with Mr. Fu.

AT THE RESTAURANT, MR. FU ORDERS the same banquet, down to the last white shrimp. Again the glass top turns, again Ling's bowl fills and empties, staining with shades of brown. One, two, three white bones appear on Mr. Fu's plate. Their second meeting passes like a recurrence of the first, so familiar it could be a dream. A waking or sleeping dream, Ling doesn't know, its quality at once of fantasy and of the subterranean. It is possible, in fact, that Ling doesn't eat a thing. Perhaps she doesn't cover her face. Perhaps she pushes her hair away and lifts her chin, saying, How can you explain this?

Mr. Fu sighs. Perhaps he spins the glass, staring at the spread, stopping every so often to pick up his chopsticks and put them down without retrieving anything to eat.

Perhaps he apologizes: I meant to tell you. I'm a coward, it's my fault.

Perhaps he orders a bottle of wine.

Or perhaps they never meet again at all. In some tellings, Ling says she is too afraid to contact Mr. Fu again, even on Baidu. Instead it is he who reaches out to her, tentative at first, then relentlessly, messaging finally: I intend to marry you. This, in all versions, is consistent. He declares his intentions clearly, without caveat, so that whoever is watching can be sure.

What exactly does Mr. Fu tell Ling, and what, in service of logic and meaning, does she invent? What exactly does Ling tell me, and what, in service of logic and meaning, do I? And what exactly compels me to return, hoping at each instance to arrive nearer to the truth?

This, somehow, is what I come to understand:

Another woman haunts Mr. Fu's life, not his ex-wife, not a lover—a childhood friend. They grew up together, attended the same schools, played in the same parks, eventually went on to the same university, not far from their childhood longtangs. She calls him Gege, like a blood sibling, and is a fiercely loyal friend. She is not unattractive, and yet she remains single, refusing marriage offers, reserving herself for him. So it is that at every major life event Mr. Fu finds her at his side: the death of his father, his sister's cancer diagnosis, the first time a woman breaks his heart. After the car accident that tears a tendon in his knee, limping him permanently, he wakes to her face over the hospital bed. How lucky he is to have a friend like this! Time after time he marvels at his good luck until it becomes a stone on his chest. Kindness is never free; he owes a great debt. And how can he repay her?

He does not want to marry her. He considers developing romantic feelings for her, how convenient it would be. He fails, again and again. He convinces himself that her interest is platonic. Even as his first marriage falls apart, he refuses to attribute it to her. After all, his ex-wife never gives him a clear reason for leaving, saying only "My life has become intolerable." Only when Mr. Fu tries to remarry does an undeniable pattern emerge. Each time a relationship progresses to a certain point, his beloved recoils, leaving him always with the same parting words.

"NOW MY LIFE," LING SAYS, "has become intolerable."

She pulls back her hair, baring the patchwork of her skin. "See?"

She takes my hand and pulls me to the unused bedroom, where she and her husband used to sleep, and shuts the door behind us. The curtains are drawn, the stacked pieces of furniture from Little Sister's demolished apartment are shadows coughing dust. She moves a nightstand and opens the closet door, gesturing, saying again, "*See?*" On the bottom shelf, I see: bottles of cooking oil, soy sauce, vinegar, salt, the lids and caps wrapped in film; above, vacuum-sealed packs of clothes.

How matters have escalated. Not just her facial cream now but every item she uses and owns is under attack. The cooking supplies in the kitchen, the clothes in her closet, the soap and shampoo in the bathroom—they are all decoys, left out for her persecutors to contaminate as they please. I look closer and see: the shadows inside the unused room have been rearranged. The dresser and bed are pulled into positions of use, the bed made and a blanket spread over two lumps shaped to mimic the human form. In the front door Ling has installed an extra lock. Even so, she can no longer leave the apartment unattended: someone might get in and spray the floors with a chemical that makes her cough and gag. Yet Hai has to go to school. Now more than ever she cannot let him walk alone. And she must leave to buy groceries, fresh groceries every day so they can't be spoiled while she sleeps. At the supermarket, she has purchased a video camera, a plastic eye the size of a child's head. Hai helps her install it—he is good with computers. On the living room table, it sits and watches the door when she can't.

Her mind is sharpening, honing, like a cold blade. It senses now when she is being followed and when she is being watched, and the leftover presence of intruders. In her apartment, outside the door, in the stairwell as she and Hai come home. Sensing, sensing, her senses are knives slicing the apparent world: if she focuses them, she can discover where her persecutors have been—the extra bedroom, the kitchen, the living room; which items—the bowls, the pillows, the toilet seat—they've soiled with ill intent. Her mind is the intelligence of her body: her body comes alive with feeling. She learns to read the small aches and discomforts in her chest, her stomach, her lungs, the minute shifts of lightness and weight in her temples and in her joints, the ghost feeling of crawling on her skin. Many times a night she wakes to the knowledge of someone standing just outside the door. She gets up and flips on the lights. She drives her persecutors away.

What a wealth of meaning life contains, just waiting to be read. Ling sees its composition now, the grains of substance that make up an image, like the pixelated displays of a surveillance tape, meaning nothing without the capacity to order them.

In her family, Little Sister is the clever one. When they were girls, Little Sister eight and Ling ten, and Father fallen ill, Little Sister was the one encouraged to continue school. Ling, on the other hand. Ling became thick, practically illiterate, a "chimpanzee in clothes," as Little Sister once said. Well, not just anyone could test into a university in Shanghai with a village education, not just anyone made it to America. Little Sister always knew how to use the substance of the world, to wield it like a tool. Ling's intelligence is of a different kind: it sees how the world wields you.

SOMETIMES, RUSHING BACK FROM THE supermarket, Ling sees her competitor. An older woman with dyed-black hair sitting outside the barbershop, across from the neighborhood gate. The woman has an angular face and sharply drawn eyebrows. She wears a dark red suit and lipstick the same venomous color. She taps her heels and glares.

Ling's chest clamps tight. A white whisper inside:

Mr. Fu, Mr. Fu.

The traffic light changes. A man follows her into the alley, turning off just before she arrives. From her entranceway emerges her neighbor like clockwork, carrying his red bag of trash. In the stairwell the whispers begin. The piano sounds in the second-floor apartment, ascending up the keyboard step by step before turning and coming down. Patterns, and their infinite tidiness: her persecutor, her persecutors. *Mr. Fu, Mr. Fu.*

Who are they, and who is he? The patches on Ling's face are real—this I can see. So she has summoned me in, to read her life, so what is boring and endless might achieve the grace of plot. Because I do pity Ling, pity her suffering and its intractability, how she's wound her life around herself in these most exquisitely fool-proof chains. I pity her so much, I envy her. Would my own mind ever be capable of such imaginative feats as these?

Ling plugs in her computer and presses the power on. She shows me the icons she clicks, twice, to go online, how she waits for the image of a computer meeting a telephone to resolve. She shows me the icon she clicks to message Mr. Fu. Today, she has called me over for a specific purpose: to examine her surveillance tape. On the computer screen I watch the grainy image of the inside of her front door. If not for the static it would be a photograph; nothing changes or moves. Only the timestamp on the top right corner ticks forward. "There!" she says. She stops the tape and rewinds. She points to the top right corner, perhaps to the timestamp, presses play, and says, "See?" She looks at me with trust, with expectation. The truth is my head is swirling. I see the raw white patching Ling's face, a sight I can't deny. I see the image on the computer screen, the closed door, the locked locks, the knob jammed by the back spokes of a chair, the towel curled neatly at the door's bottom seam. I see Hai at the kitchen table bent over a sheet of sums. Pieces that almost add up to a story.

Ling insists. She says the tape has been altered, taped over, a manufactured image inserted to hide the truth. How did they do it, she wants to know, and can I restore the original? I know nothing about recording equipment. I pick up the device. The supermarket camera is plastic and round, like the bulbous eye of a fantastical one-eyed beast. Her "surveillance system"—I must stifle a pained laugh—looks like a child's toy.

I am holding the eye, staring back, when Ling stands up in alarm. "You have to go," she says, and pushes me out the door.

THE PATCHES ARE REAL. AND SO is the rest: the people, the places, the visions, the suffering most of all. I change names because I cannot bear it otherwise. And there are the lacunae of memory, of logic, of my own failures of understanding. Whenever I invent I do so to serve meaning, to distort, with my ugly writer's hand, what is insufferable into that which might be contained. I am not proud of this. But given an incomplete set of observations, it is what I know how to do.

For months Ling remains frozen in place. Weekly she messages Mr. Fu. She wants to prove to him she can tolerate the intolerable, that no pain surpasses her will to life. Weathering the torment not only proves her a worthy wife, it proves her ability to survive.

Then, one afternoon, the phone rings. It is Hai's school. Her son has left class and is in the office, ill. She arrives at the school, hair pulled back and sweating. Hai crouches on the floor, body curled in a knot, crying stomachache, an ache so intense he cannot stand. Crying, when he has been too big to cry for years.

At the hospital, scans show his pancreas swollen to twice its normal size. Digestion of any food results in excruciating pain. The doctors keep him in bed, running tests and feeding him nothing but saline from a bag. A day passes, two, three. Ling sits by his bed day and night. Still the doctors cannot find a source for the disease. His arms grow so thin they look like they might snap. His little neck barely holds up his head. The second week of his hospital stay, he begins to talk in his sleep. One night, he wakes and calls for Ling.

What happened to Baba? he says. Did he die like this?

Ling says, Don't be silly.

THE NEXT MORNING SHE WILL go home, protecting her face with a scarf, and open the drawer of Little Sister's red envelopes. She will not count the cash inside. At the temple, before the plaque with her husband's name, she will make a final offering. By then, she will already have messaged Mr. Fu.

I surrender, she will write. Please don't contact me again.

When she returns to the hospital Hai's swelling will recede, and the next day, he will be discharged.

HAI'S BABA WAS A COWARD. A giant but afraid of everything, she almost smiles to remember. How he never tells her, before or after they marry and have a child, that he is sick, sick in the heart, so sick he must take medicine every day just to want to survive. The pills he swallows with breakfast: for high blood pressure, he says. A big man, indulging in fatty foods—she believes he has high blood pressure. Husband, Mother-in-Law, Sister-in-Law, entire Husband's family conspires to keep the medicine's true purpose a secret from her. Day after day, for three years, as she makes their meals and mops their floors and wrings out their laundry to dry, as she carries their descendant and births him, Husband and Mother-in-Law look her in the eye and let her live a lie. No wonder everyone from every side hurried them into marriage. Little Sister says Ling is lucky, nearing thirty with no education and a countryside hukou, to land a Shanghai man with a steady job, even if he is a little fat and a little lazy. Ling doesn't learn the truth about her husband's disease until the day she comes home from the market and finds his body bloated and dead on the kitchen floor.

The kitchen is small and he is large. His swollen arms are wedged underneath the cabinet doors. She tries to pry him out. She shouts but no sound comes from her mouth. Light-headed, spinning, as if lifted by an invisible force, she rises and runs to the windows, opening each as wide as it will go. She turns on the ceiling fan, the A/C. It is February. The sky is a bright Shanghai gray. She pulls the floor fan out from the closet and plugs it in. She leans out the bathroom window, gasping, gasping.

He plans it so she is the one to find him. He closes the kitchen door. He pulls the window tight and seals the cracks with towels. He makes sure the gas tank is full. He makes sure the baby is gone. That morning, Mother-in-Law takes Hai to see Sister-in-Law, who lives on the other side of Shanghai. Later, when Ling begins to understand, she thanks the heavens that at least he has enough courage for this.

No, she finally tells Hai in his hospital bed, Baba didn't die like this. Baba didn't suffer. He wasn't strong, like us.

"The hallucinatory quality of grief"—

Words I've underlined in my notes. "Death," Ling wants to tell me, "is the one certainty of life. The one thing every person can be sure to accomplish, regardless of circumstances of birth."

And yet, eight years after her husband gave up, Ling still cannot believe it. She knows it, sure. Without much effort she can conjure the body, the swollen toes purpling under the lip of the stove. He isn't around, hasn't been for years. His absence at the dinner table, on the other side of the bed, the lack of his boxer shorts hanging on the balcony to dry: facts. Yet the knowledge of this death, so many years later, remains abstract, so abstract it is like forgetting. She calls herself a widow, yes, a widow is what she is. But she does not, cannot, think of herself as a woman whose husband has chosen to die. Not really. If she allows this vision, if she sees herself, truly, as another might, she will dissolve with pity—shock—scorn.

WHEN I LAST MEET LING, it is spring. She is throwing open her windows, unlocking her doors, taking gulps of fresh air into her lungs. Her child is healthy and safe. For once she seems happy, free, spiritually unguarded, the pieces of her settled into something like a self—though Ling would say, "Self, what self, what kind of nonsense is that?"—and it is in this state that I find her consciousness, tossed on the back of a chair, like a jacket gratefully shed in the warmth of one's own home. I try it on; it finally suits me. I take it for my own.

Self-Portrait with Ghost

> Immediately she trusted me, put my past behind
> her, wiped the record clean.
>
> —Grace Paley, "Wants"

I saw Gugu in the street. She was sitting on the bench outside the public library.

What are you doing here? I said. She had been dead for sixteen years. Even when she was alive, she had never crossed the ocean to see me, though not out of malice or disregard. I know she'd meant more to me than I had to her. She'd meant more to me because for so long, she had pursued death with a near religious fervor. She was the first person of that type I'd known.

She looked at me sullenly. I might have expected death to change her, to fill her, perhaps, with a light so abundant it could be shared. But she looked just as she had the last time I'd seen her, twenty-odd years ago in Jinhua: chubby-cheeked and slow-moving, as if in an aquarium, her hair cropped close like a boy's. She was wearing slippers and a long blue robe, like she was still afraid to leave the house.

I guess I wanted to see what you were reading, she said. Nowadays, I mean, now that you're a writer.

I said, Okay. I opened my backpack for her to see. Inside were two monographs on traditional Chinese poetics, one through the lens of memory and the other through the lens of place, and an art book on Song dynasty landscape painting. They were written by men named James and Stephen, the kind of books whose mere existence had for years intimidated or infuriated me or both. They were heavy. My back was sweating from carrying them up the hill in the full sun.

They're in English, Gugu said regretfully, fingering through the pages. I guess you never learned how to express yourself properly in Chinese.

I realized then that Gugu was speaking in English, a language she didn't know. I felt at once grateful and ashamed. I had had these books for six months and still hadn't read them. They were twice overdue. I had planned to return them so I could check them out again, which was allowed only because no one else in this city of readers wanted them. According to the catalog cards in the back pockets, they hadn't been touched in sixteen years.

The power of painting, Gugu read out loud, is to function as a substitute for the thing it represents, by arousing in the viewer those emotions that the actual scene would arouse. The forms of nature possess not only physical substance but immaterial qualities of *attractiveness* or *flavor*; and it is by these qualities, rather than by outward appearances, that the spirit of the sensitive man is affected.

She turned to me: Very interesting. You know, the more you write, the more I can see that unlike me, you are fundamentally uninterested in the difference between reality and unreality.

But my novel was all about subjectivity, I said. Each character tells their version of reality and the various realities add up to something that looks more like unknowing than a solution. And what about that story with the ambiguous "I," or the one about paranoid grief, or the one set in a city that is kind of like this one but not? In all of them reality shifts somehow to question the very nature of what we privilege as real.

She stood up and walked to the book return bin. She was limping slightly, as she had been when last I saw her. This puzzled me. By the time she'd succeeded in dying, the injury from that attempt must have been long healed. I moved to help her but she continued on without pause. With a smooth motion, as if she had done it many times before, she slid the books into the metal mouth one by one.

I tried not to mourn the books. I could still read them. Whenever I desired, I could request them on an online portal, and within days they'd be delivered to my neighborhood branch. If I wanted to, I could go inside now and ask the librarian to retrieve them from the bin. The public library was a benevolent institution; already it had forgiven me without fuss for what others might not: absence, neglect, coming only when it suited me and usually in the service of some stupid story.

Remember that story you made up, Gugu said, in the summer of 1999?

I was surprised. It had been one of many unglamorous hours after lunch, when we were supposed to be asleep. The girls were shut in the air-conditioned room: Gugu at the computer, playing her games, while her four-year-old daughter and I goofed off on the bamboo bed. The story itself was a derivative collage of narratives pilfered from Saturday-morning cartoons, an inane tale about a crazed mouse who robs a piano shop. That was all I remembered about it, and how when the police, searching for the culprit, questioned bystanders for leads, they were met with incredulous stares. A mouse? reasonable people asked. Why would a mouse want a piano?

It was such an accomplished story, Gugu said. Funny, gripping, springing fully formed from the imagination. At the time I thought you might have a talent for writing. Now I wonder if I pushed you the wrong way.

I was very impressionable, I said.

In fact, at age ten, I'd been exhilarated to hear Gugu call me a writer, though I knew enough not to repeat it to other adults. You can't trust Gugu, they'd have said, or: Do you want to end up like her? Even her daughter had rolled her eyes, tugging my arm for the next story. But Gugu's praise brimmed in my throat; for decades it stifled me.

I wanted to keep the realms separate, she said. But you conflate them with abandon.

I said, That's unfair. I try to be deliberate.

It's not enough, she said. From my vantage the status of the real and unreal is totally clear. One exists, and the other is dangerous. There is no thinning of boundaries. A reality that is really in flux is a state of terror. You can complain about the rigidity of contemporary life but it's thinking like yours that creates problems.

Like that, she started to walk away. I sat down on the bench where I'd found her and considered her accusations. It was true that I felt strongly about human experience not falling neatly into binaries. It was true, perhaps, that this way of seeing made light of how Gugu had lived and died. But I had never intended to offend her.

I watched her limp up the block, up another hill. I'd had so many questions I wanted to ask; instead, I'd wasted all my time defending myself. I wondered, for instance, if pain still hurt her. I wondered if in death, she contained every version of herself she'd been in life. Was she limping now, in my vision, only because I'd known her that way? How would she have appeared if, like my grandmother or father, I'd known her when she was well?

I wondered if, when she spoke now about the things she saw and heard, she was still called crazy. I imagined ghosts were more charitable. I imagined Gugu sitting around a fire with new acquaintances, speaking her strange mind. The other ghosts would laugh and nod in appreciation, or they would shake their heads in sympathy. In either case they would accept her stories at face value without questioning which parts were real and which parts were fake, at least not in a narrow sense.

There you go again, Gugu said, and I heard her voice as clearly as if she were still standing beside me.

Right, I said. I was falling back into the same patterns of thought she had just exposed.

How would you write this, then, I asked, if you were me?

She didn't respond. She was far away now, her body cresting the hill and starting to disappear down its other side. It was an unseasonably hot day. Insects buzzed in the tufts of grass lining the sidewalks, and the ridges of the mountains in the distance shimmered from the heat. Gugu was a black smudge shrinking in the haze of afternoon light. I thought of the books inside the bin, which might help me see things differently, which might free me, even, from the muddling instincts of postmodernity. I stood up and started after her. Wait for me, I called out. I walked briskly, but no longer in a hurry.

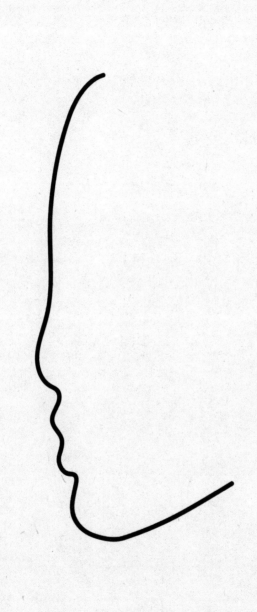

Three Women

1

There were three women I remember—three girls. Though they appeared like women to me, like they were—complete. I was a girl: most days I played with a doll made of cloth scraps at the foot of my grandmother's sewing machine. I was always in her hair—my grandmother's. Always she looked at me with her forehead folded in irritation. Later I learned she couldn't help it. That angry wrinkle between her eyes was a scar she'd had since she was a girl herself—not from a lifetime spent frowning. She never would tell me what the scar was from.

When my grandmother smiled, it was because one of the three women—girls—had come to the door.

"Thank god—look at these orders—look how she's tangled the thread—go, bless you—don't buy her any candy, not even if she begs—that one's got a rotten tooth."

Oh, I loved those days too. Next thing, I'd be in the park, or on the back of a bicycle, elbows wrapped around a soft waist, the busy wind whipping the ties from my hair. "Jiejie!" I'd cry—I called them all Jiejie—"It's so much fun!" And she would reply, "Hold on tight now," or "Good to enjoy while you're little," or, if it was the wicked one, the one I wanted to grow up to be, she'd just cackle and stand up on the pedals, charging forward at speed.

On her bicycle, I sat on the handlebars, laughing, holding on for dear life, as her long hair—never braided—flew around my face, mixing with her salty, grown-up girl scent.

It was a pleasurable game to ask myself, when I was bored at home with Grandmother, which jiejie I loved most. There was the wicked one, of course. She was the one I envied, though she wasn't the prettiest or cleverest, because I was a coward, obsessively obedient—like a good girl ought to be: I wished I could be brave. She had a narrow face like an olive, a sprinkle of freckles across her nose, and eyes that, when they weren't winking at me, could turn hard as a black stone. Unafraid, she winked as we ran past the park monitor without paying, as she slipped a candy into my pocket at the grocer's, as she palmed the coins left uncounted at the noodle stall counter.

Three women—girls—one was wicked, one was good. The good one was also pretty. You couldn't hate her for being pretty because she was pretty on the inside too. Her rosy smile, her shiny black hair, cut short and neat just below her chin, her warm and twinkling eyes—all those lovely features seemed like nothing else but the true manifestation of her soul. She hugged me and I couldn't help but smile. She was everybody's favorite, including my grandmother's. My grandmother who mended clothes for the building, muttering as she pumped the sewing machine, took care with the pretty one's clothes. "Well this didn't even fit properly, I'll fix that," she'd say, or "How nice this color will look on her." My grandmother sewed dresses for the jiejies with leftover cloth, in exchange for looking after me—she saved the nicest fabrics for the pretty one.

The wicked and pretty ones came to my grandmother's door in town. The third one I didn't see unless we went to the village. She was a cousin, I think, somehow related—everybody in the village was. Unfailingly she appeared at the door with a gift for my grandmother and a gift for me—unfailingly she took my hand before I reached out for hers. I didn't like her, I didn't like the smell of her skin—on the back of her bicycle I sniffed and thought: flesh. Was she pretty or ugly? I can't remember. In my mind she was only the third one, the boring one.

The boring one, because she spoke to me like a teacher. She said, "See how your grandmother works so hard, perhaps you can learn to sew and help her," or "Pluck the best pieces of meat for your grandmother, the elderly need good nutrition." She reminded me to greet every relative we saw with the proper address. Always telling me how to be good, a good and honorable girl, but really she was sweet to me because my mother was in America, and she wanted to go there too. She tried to be like the pretty one, I thought, but you could see it wasn't honest, and she wasn't wild enough to be like the wicked one either. Perhaps I didn't like her because she was just like me.

She was the only one of the three who wasn't in love.

"She's beautiful because she's in love"—years later, my mother said this; perhaps she was talking about me. The pretty one was in love. I met her boyfriend many times: he was just as good and pretty as she. They were both planning to go to university in the big city come fall. One day they took me on a bus out of town, more than an hour away, so far away I thought we were going to the city. But where we got off it looked more like the village, a beautiful version, or perhaps I just thought this because Jiejie exclaimed, "How beautiful the mountains are!"

"Everything looks beautiful when you're in love"—my mother liked to say this too.

Stairs had been laid going up the mountain, and we climbed to the very top. Jiejie's boyfriend carried a bag full of snacks, stewed tea eggs and sunflower seeds and little sausages he peeled from red plastic casings for me. Near the top he picked me up, placed me on his shoulders, and jogged the final stretch. "Careful!" Jiejie protested, so he put me down and threw her over his shoulder instead. At the summit I found them laughing, out of breath. That was the day I saw, for the first time, a man and woman kiss. I thought about Jiejie's sweet lips, red with excitement, and her cold hands around his neck. Afterward her face was flushed. She had forgotten about me—I must have stood there gaping. She took my hand and said, "Don't worry, we're getting married next year."

The wicked one never said anything about getting married. She was in love with too many boys, every boy we met she introduced as "the love of my life," or, when she was in a mischievous mood, "my husband." Many times we were with all her husbands at once. There was a house we visited, in the crowded alleyways behind the People's Square, where the husbands gathered, sitting outside and playing cards or crowded around the television in the living room, smoking cigarettes. We were the only girls and this made us feel special. The husbands had a language of their own, looks and silences and gestures of the shoulders and neck: it exhilarated me to sit and watch, as if I had been let in on a secret. Jiejie didn't just speak their language. She seemed to control it, directing the movements of her husbands like an orchestra master waving his hands. I never saw her kiss anyone, but often she had an arm slung around her shoulders or waist, and when one of the husbands annoyed her, she'd twist his ear and scold him, eyes narrowed, mouth an inch from his. She'd pluck a cigarette from his lips and suck in a mouthful of smoke. She was the only girl I'd ever seen with a cigarette between her teeth.

"Sit here like a good wife," one of them said, patting his knees.

She snapped back: "Watch who you're calling wife, old man."

That day she was wearing a white skirt cut above her knees and a blouse that showed her bare shoulders. Whenever I remember her, these are the clothes she's wearing. Her skirt is slightly rumpled, creased at the hem, and her black hair falls like a curtain, draping loose over her shoulders and back.

She gathered the curtain and twisted it into a bun. She dropped her hands and let it all tumble down. Every eye was glued to her.

The husband put his hand on her leg. He held it awkwardly, dug his fingers in. "Be a good wife," he said, "stop blocking the TV." He coughed a laugh—he pulled her onto his lap.

Nobody was watching the TV. The contradiction of his words lit a wire in the room. I was alert, alive, suddenly electric, with the kind of excitement I imagined men felt before a fight—I wanted my hand around Jiejie's leg, or—and—his hand around my leg too. Then the room was shifting. The boys were standing up and moving about in a flurry of unfocused activity, and I could no longer see Jiejie over their heads. One of them told another one, the youngest, to go buy some more cigarettes and take me—"Go to the shop on Renmin Lu," he said, and I thought, But that one's so far away! I found myself at the shop, the youngest boy slipping a box of cigarettes into his pocket, looking at me like he was sorry. He bought me a strawberry candy. When we got back it was melting on my tongue.

2

"I used to think China hated women, but America hates women even more," the third one said, many years later. Her name was Tian. A romantic name, I thought, and I almost liked her for it. We were being reintroduced in my mother's American living room. Quickly she corrected me: not tian like *sky* but tian like *sweet*. So I was to call her Sweet Elder Sister. I refused the mooncake she offered. "I can't stand red bean," I said. "I can't stand sweets."

Some years ago Tian had become an American—now she was a Chinese nationalist. She loved to compare her countries. "Do Americans have more freedom than the Chinese?" she asked rhetorically. "China has lifted millions from poverty, while America's poverty rate is increasing every day." Or, "The problem with this kind of democracy . . . the dream of progress is never actually achieved." Sometimes she cast her scales more broadly: "Americans are lazy and care only for themselves; Chinese are industrious and love their country."

By the time I left China, the jiejies had stopped coming to the door. I'd looked at the open frame, waiting for a face to appear. Full of hope and expectation—I had memories of promises, the wicked one and the good one and probably Tian too, saying, "I'll bring a gift for you to remember me by."

My mother came; the women didn't. I imagined what they were doing and sometimes I spoke my imaginings out loud. "She's married." "She's gone off to university, she's learning everything there is to learn." "Can we go to her wedding, she'll be happy to see me, I know it, please?" My grandmother shushed me. I resigned myself—the jiejies had forgotten me. I went with my mother and forgot them too.

"She was so pretty," my grandmother said once, regretfully.

Or maybe that was later, when I returned to visit, almost a woman myself. About the wicked one my grandmother had no shortage of words. "That one's gone sour—ripened too soon—her poor mother—I'd be heartbroken too. No, I'd be firm, that's the problem—her mother's too soft, if it were me I'd turn her out of the house."

Tian said Mao's China freed women from vanity, made them the same as men. "No one questioned if your mother or I could work office jobs like our husbands." Then women were freed from being beasts of carriage; since the eighties China had birth controls and abortions plenty, no questions asked, because of the one-child policy. It wasn't like in America, where people threw pig's blood on women who didn't want a child, where desperate girls went into back alleys with rusty clothes hangers and bled out onto the concrete. Mao's China was atheist, governed by science, unlike America, which was governed by Christian fanatics. Americans believed man was created in the image of God. Americans believed God had to bless their country. Chinese understood progress was up to the citizens and leaders. Social planning, Tian said, was a science too.

"Only the older generation is stuck in the old ways," she concluded sadly. Her mother wanted a grandson to carry on the family name, scolded Tian for not having a son; after all, she lived in America, the land of Christian fanatics, where the child-bearing was plentiful; in the village her mother hung her head in shame. "She can't help it," Tian said, repeating, "She's stuck in the old ways."

Tian had a daughter. The girl was seven years old, a replica of her mother: forgettable-faced, smiling meekly and enthusiastically at once. She was dressed like a schoolgirl with a red bow in her hair. "No need to call me Jiejie," I told her, "call me by my name." I pulled on her bow and her braid unraveled. There was another girl inside, I was almost certain, dying to break out.

"WHY DOESN'T SHE JUST HAVE a second child?"—me, impertinent.

"Oh, she's probably trying, and she doesn't know she can't"—my mother, indifferent.

What my mother meant was, probably she had gotten pregnant after having her daughter, before she came to America. Then, when she'd had the abortion, her tubes had been tied for future ease.

"That's what happened to me, anyways."

"You had an abortion?"

"You had a little brother."

Then: "Don't worry. I always wanted a girl."

I WAS A COLLEGE STUDENT. I was interested in my mind and rarely considered my body. When people said, "Her body did not belong to her," I filled my eyes with sorrow because my mind determined I should. I didn't really know what they meant. Could a body belong to anyone, including oneself?

I wanted to learn how to love boys. I paid attention when girls talked. I looked carefully at boys, at their faces and bodies, learned them like flash cards. This one was "cute" and also "hot." This one was "a babe." This one was "sweet" and "nice," but you didn't "like him like that." It was so much work, determining if a boy was to be wanted, to be loved. Whereas it was clear as day with girls. I could look at a girl and instantly say if she was ugly or pretty, beautiful or gorgeous, if she was plain but sweet, if I wanted to look like her or not. If I envied her, if I could dream myself into her body. I couldn't see my own body unless I was looking at it beside another girl's. A quick study, I quickly discovered an easy way to tell about a boy: if his girlfriend was pretty or not.

3

"Who's that?"

"You don't recognize her?"

I looked closer, and then I did. Still closer, and the recognition reversed. The woman looked like the imitation of someone I'd known, or perhaps the leftover. Like a memory had been sketched but not colored in.

"Is she . . ."

"The wicked girl you idolized. She turned out all right."

I would not have picked her from a crowd. My eyes would have passed over, dismissing. What I mean is she looked incredibly dull, like anybody.

"And who are they?"

"Her husband, her son."

"He's nearly as tall as me!"

"She's lucky his family agreed to marry. Her reputation in those days! The child could have been anybody's. Well, they were satisfied when it turned out to be a son. Don't you think he looks like his father?"

His father, the husband, looked exactly as he had on the day he grabbed her leg. It was summer then, just as it was summer now. The town was changed. The bicycles had become motorcycles, and the old stalls selling lamb skewers were now offering electronic repairs. My grandmother's hair had turned totally white but otherwise she looked the same.

The woman and the husband were sitting beside each other on a park bench, sitting just as they had on that afternoon. She with purposeful boredom; he with his jaw slack, relaxed.

That afternoon, she had looked relieved to see me. She had reached out her hand, and I took it. I sat on her other side. For the rest of the day we'd stared in silence at the TV, Jiejie gripping my hand tightly, so tightly I felt her pulse in my palm. I was confused—the room seemed crowded, like it had shrunk. I had the strange feeling that while I was gone getting cigarettes and candy the boys had been swapped for different versions of themselves. Still I could not help but be exhilarated by Jiejie's proximity, and by the feeling of a new secret growing. I pressed my head against Jiejie's arm. I saw, bewildered, that instead of her white skirt she was wearing pants. They were loose, ugly, gray—men's pants. I took my hand out of hers and touched them, touched her leg, just to see if they were real. She said, "Dear Meimei, don't," and her voice trailed off.

"She turned out all right," my grandmother said again.

I wanted to be cheered up. In my memory the town was vibrant, loud, happy; in my first lonely years in America I had missed it terribly. Now it was dusty and poor and hot. I wanted something to be better than I remembered.

"Where's the pretty one," I asked, "the one you loved? The one—you said I should be just like her."

My grandmother picked up her pace. I stumbled behind her, leaning in to catch what bits I could of her sudden muttering. She was speaking in dialect, one of many things I'd forgotten; I understood a quarter of what she said.

"... abandoned ... child ... so pitiful! Refused to ... loved so much ... who else would marry? ... mother threatened ... gave it up ... found her hanging."

"She's dead?"

"No, no ... lost in the head ... unmarried ... gave up the girl for what! ... sweet fool."

She brightened and switched to Mandarin:

"We can go visit her if you like. She's still pretty, fatter now, her cheeks are big like a baby's. She still lives with her parents in the old building, we can take that road over there. No? Should we invite the other one to dinner? You were so fond of her, she was always your favorite. She turned out all right. Her husband's the head of his neighborhood committee I hear, not bad, though he lost some money gambling. It's no trouble to invite them, we'll go over and do it now, you remember she was good to you, and I never did make that dress. Yes, she turned out all right, she's married and—no? But your uncle could talk to her husband about—"

"No!"

AT COLLEGE THE FOLLOWING FALL, I met an extraordinarily beautiful girl. She had hair and skin so light she almost disappeared, but her eyes—they were very green. Otherworldly, I thought when I watched her. We played in the chamber orchestra together. I don't know if she knew my name.

One night I saw her at a party. I had imagined her as very pure, saintly even, as she bowed her violin, but now I saw her throwing back plastic cup after cup of beer. Her arms flew around a boy, their hips locked together as they danced. In the dark, I stood across the room staring and biting my tongue. She kissed him, and when she took her lips back, their imprint remained on his. I encountered a revelation then, a knowledge seeping warmly: here was a boy, a beautiful boy; I was starting to understand how to want him. She grabbed his face and kissed him again. His hands moved over her body, one took a breast and the other a leg, just above her hem at the knee. Dancing and kissing, soon they went down the hall to his room—his room, I knew, because not a week later I made my way there too, certain that this was where I would find my body, find her and take possession over her, so that one day a person might look at me and say, "She belonged to herself, and no one else."

First Love

The train from the city to the country was slow and long and cost more than I could afford, but it was worth it to see X. Anything was worth it then. I was thoroughly in love, so much so that all I could think about day in and day out was what love meant, why it existed, what it was good for. I didn't like being in love. After all my thinking I came up with nothing useful, except perhaps that love made children, which kept the human race alive. But love also made people crazy—it made me crazy. In love, I acted totally against my nature and against my best sense. I knew it but I couldn't help it. When I wasn't with X, every part of me wanted only to be with him, and when I was with him, even when we weren't having a fabulous time, I forgot that there might exist any other purpose in life.

Usually I could find a seat. It helped that I had the baby with me. If I stood over some young fellow, holding the girl in one arm and my purse in the other, eventually he would offer me his place. Sometimes he would comment on the child, asking how old she was (almost a year), what was her name (Guagua, see how her head is round like a melon), complimenting me on her beauty and obedience. Look how she never cries! I would nod gratefully like the exhausted mother I was pretending to be.

"She's healthy, thank god," I'd say with a look of relief. Or, on the journey back to the city, "Let's pray it's just a cough."

Most people with children on the train were taking them to or from the municipal hospital. But the girl wasn't sick and she wasn't mine. I was just a negligent nanny, taking advantage of the child's easy temperament and inability to speak to do with my days as I pleased.

My relief, however, was real: soon I would see X.

On that day, the train was particularly full. As if my lies had manifested, the seats in every compartment were occupied by real mothers carrying their real children, many of whom were still dressed in the hospital's drab blue skullcaps and face masks. I found an empty corner and leaned against it, holding on to the rail. For the duration of the ride, I stood there as Guagua clawed at my hair and spat up, nearly soiling my new blouse. Overcome with motion sickness myself, I wanted badly to sit on the floor, but it was splattered with her milky puke. So I stood there unhappily, collecting my unhappiness for the arsenal of indignities I was always assembling for some unknown future purpose.

It wouldn't be too long before I found use for this one. When Guagua was big enough to understand—big enough to complain about the little one who'd taken her place, my own child, a son—I'd tell her about this journey. She despised my son. She'd pull at my pants and ask, "Why do you hold him all the time? Doesn't he know how to eat food? He's so stupid, he can't even say ma-ma." And once, "Did you feed me from your breast too?" I'd remind her of her own once-uselessness: "How my arms ached! How heavy you were, much heavier than him." How I've suffered for you, my face would say; to suffer for someone would be by then how I'd learned to love.

When she asked where I'd been taking her, I'd say without missing a beat, "To see your grandparents, stupid. Now finish your soup."

The train pulled in; I looked out the windows for X. I liked to see him before he saw me, to see the expression on his face before it set into the one he made. There he was, standing behind a cage of chickens, hands clasped, neck straining toward the train door. On his face was the look that mirrored my own, one between despondence and hope, the open hope of not knowing yet that the other had come. I stepped into the doorway and waved. He came forward, stacking his smile into something more manly and reserved, and stopped an arm's length away. He eyed the collar of my blouse where the red silk fell against my neck. He had given me this blouse, wrapped in a plastic sleeve, for my birthday; for weeks I had waited for the weather to warm to wear it. Now suddenly I felt embarrassed, immodest, I was wearing my desire like a flag.

He took the child from me.

"How pretty you look, like a plum," he said, and I was so happy.

X WORKED IN A FURNITURE parts factory in Shanghe, the town at the end of the train line. From there you could take a bus to the village where we'd all been born, where our families still lived. Technically I still lived there too. In the city I slept on a cot in my employer's living room, shared with the baby; weekends and holidays I took the train and bus back to my family house to sleep on the dirt floor where I'd slept for all of my life.

I liked meeting X outside of the village. We had grown up together, running up the mountains barefoot, jumping into the pond and crawling out covered in mud. X was the head of the group— the oldest, strongest, wildest—and I was the tail, the smallest follower, sprinting to catch up. He never noticed or spoke to me. I liked being a follower—I liked following X, who was always in movement, unbound, running carefree over the horizon. Then we got too big to play with boys. I started going to school, and at home, learning my mother's chores. I washed and hung my brothers' muddy clothes, I scalded my fingers with hot oil, I hunted for firewood on the tamed paths, while a small fold inside my awareness, tucked between the heart and the stomach, continued to watch X from afar.

In Shanghe, I was a discovery: a young woman he'd found looking for the train platform on her first day going to the city for work. "Meimei," he'd said, "I know you," and he did and he didn't.

The station had lit up. It had been years since I had last seen X. His wiry frame had filled in, the playful expression on his boy face had set into permanent grooves and lines. I laughed. He told me he didn't know a single person in Shanghe, and said he'd like to see me again. As in childhood, the horizon had spooled open. I was starting a dreadful job, yes, but I would pass through here twice a week. For a hot moment I believed that taking this job in the city might actually change my life, as everyone seemed to think.

For months I saw X at the train station, sometimes letting him buy me breakfast, smiling silently as he implored me again and again to come back someday for lunch. I tried not to seem too eager. When I finally relented, arriving on the noon train, he took me to a shiny cafeteria in the busy town center where the cups and bowls were wrapped in plastic and ordered more food than we could eat—more food, I *thought*, than we could eat. X slurped and chewed with a joyful ease, until every plate was clean. He ate and spoke and moved without any of the hesitation and enforced humility of my—what I'd once believed to be *our*—upbringing.

In spite of myself I came back, weekly, sometimes more than once, arriving always by the noon train. Sometimes we'd stroll down the main street looking in the shop windows, where X pointed out if there was something new to buy. Some days we paid a yuan to walk around the park, and once, we climbed the seven-story pagoda together, X carrying Guagua on his shoulders. On our way down, he pulled me into the dark corner of a stairwell and kissed me. It was the first time anyone had kissed me, and I was so surprised, so elated probably, that afterward I couldn't remember a thing.

He kissed me often after that. I kissed him too, hungrily, pressing for the lost memory of that first time.

THAT DAY, X WAS NERVOUS and oddly formal, holding himself stiffly, not speaking much except to say, every few minutes, "We're nearly there," or "Just another turn." I followed him in silence as he turned down narrow streets. Over his shoulder the baby tracked me like a target, gurgling nonsense noises, her voice rising in pitch when she momentarily lost sight of me around a corner.

Guagua was a watchful child. She liked especially to watch people—to watch me. I imagined she watched me because after all this time she was not sure who exactly I was, how exactly I was different from her mother, if I was a separate person or one of the many manifestations her mother took. I fed her, I bathed her, I held her, all the things her mother used to do and probably still did on the weekends, when I disappeared. Her mother and I were of a similar stature, both short and compact, with chubby arms and generous chests. How was Guagua to understand: Her mother changed clothes, couldn't she change faces too? Guagua had a calm, sometimes even sweet temperament, rarely crying unless something truly upset her. One of those things was see-ing her mother and me at the same time. Whoever was holding her, she would reach out to the other, inconsolable; we'd pass her wailing body back and forth, going mad with attempts to distract her; she wouldn't be comforted until one of us left the room.

Finally X and I entered a gray residential building at the edge of town. I followed X up the stairs and down an echoey hall. He ducked into a room that was barely big enough for the bunk bed and chest of drawers inside it. All the furniture had been pushed to the far corner, and at the center a small folding table had been set for two.

"What's this?" I said.

"Shanghe's finest restaurant."

I laughed.

"My roommate is away for the week, I wanted to do something special for you." He put Guagua down on the bottom bunk and gestured for me to sit.

"No, she crawls now, put her on the floor."

He did so, then turned to the window, where a pot simmered over a small coal stove. He brought over two bowls of something gray and lumpy and wet.

"I'm afraid the noodles got soggy." He was grinning guiltily, handsomely.

"It looks horrible," I said, laughing.

We sat looking at the bowls and each other, neither of us reaching for our spoons. I felt that X was waiting for something, that he had something he wanted to say. Then his face was an inch from mine, and he was kissing me, kissing me as he never had before, long and deeply, so I didn't just feel it on my lips but all the way down through my lungs and stomach, in some organ that was just now waking into existence. His hands held my waist, tight, and he pulled me up, nudged the chair aside with his leg, all the while opening my mouth with his tongue. He moved his hands underneath the red blouse, and his fingers pressed on my bare skin. Then I was on my back, on the bed, my blouse un-buttoned, and he was everywhere, I was swimming in him. He kissed my breasts and my belly and said, "Do you love me?" and I must have said, *Yes, I love you*, or perhaps I said nothing at all because I felt the words were written on my skin.

All of a sudden he retreated. I blinked. He was kneeling over me, looking away. He moved and slumped at the edge of the bed. I sat up, holding my blouse closed, my chest suddenly cold, the memory of his touch already flying out the open window. I'd barely had time to register what was happening. It's gone, I thought regretfully, and wondered when he would touch me and kiss me like that again.

He was looking at the child. Guagua looked back at him—us—with an expression of puzzled interest.

"It's too strange, with the baby."

"I'll come back without her," I blurted.

"Is it possible?"

"Yes, this Saturday."

"I can't on Saturday." His face fell, then brightened. "But next Tuesday—can you? Peng comes back on Wednesday." He paused, smoothing my hair. "I'll make you proper food—I'll buy a cake from the Western bakery. It'll be this big, covered all over in white cream and roses, I'll feed it to you myself."

We sat for some moments at the edge of the bed, staring at Guagua staring at us.

"She looks like her mother, don't you think?" he said.

"What?" I hadn't known X knew who the child's mother was.

"Dong Yun, right? Doesn't she work for that new company in the city, the one manufacturing electronic chips?"

I shrugged. Hastily, I buttoned my blouse, snatched up Guagua, and returned to the table. "At least I don't have to chew this for her," I said, spooning the noodle mush into her mouth.

X sat down and began to eat. "This is disgusting," he said.

My bowl was already half-empty, the baby eating obediently, too much. She was a greedy girl, already she knew how to survive, like her mother. I put down the spoon and stood up.

"Aren't you hungry?"

"I have to catch the train."

"I'll walk you."

"You have to get back to work."

Like that I was out, storming down the lane in the direction of the train station. "Next Tuesday," X shouted behind me, his voice a plea, "I'll be waiting for you!" I picked up my pace.

At the station, I sat on the platform, waiting for X to reappear. Come back, he'd say, or, I miss you. Perhaps he'd offer to take the afternoon off, perhaps he'd offer to hire me a car. My stomach growled. The train came clanging in. I picked up the baby and got on.

GUAGUA'S MOTHER WAS A FRIEND. That's what I said when I ran into anyone I knew: "A favor for a friend in the city." Really Dong was my employer, and in her mind, she was the one doing me a favor. Some years ago my father had developed a nasty cough, a sound like the wind whacking his throat, and when he finally went to the hospital they told us it was cancer in the lungs. We couldn't afford to keep seeing the doctor for something like cancer, nobody could. By then my brothers had proved themselves useless, Da Ge gambling away his income and Er Ge scrambling to marry a pretty girl he'd gotten pregnant before he even had a job. What great fortune that Dong called when she did, how good of her to think of us. That's what my mother said. My mother, when she saw Dong these days, clutched her hands and spoke in a tone of grateful supplication, as if Dong were the Guanyin pusa incarnate.

It was true that Dong and I had been friends once, a long time ago. In primary school, for five years until I dropped out, we were inseparable. In the mornings, I'd run over to her house across the pond and we'd walk the three kilometers to the schoolhouse. We ate lunch together, splitting our pickled greens—she liked the leafy parts, I liked the stems—we copied each other's homework and played after school in the courtyard behind her house until the first smoke of dinner rose from the chimneys. But our lives took very different turns. Or hers did: mine stayed exactly where it had been. She went on to university, married a rich man, and moved to the city, where she got a job that paid her to sit in an office all day. She and her husband made so much money sitting in offices, they could pay other people to do all their work for them: the cooking, the cleaning, the mothering.

When she'd first called, she had spoken with sentimentality. "How could I forget," she'd said, "the affection between us?" I swallowed. For a while the baby had been sent to Dong's parents in the village, but Guagua had gotten sick there, malnourished and a feast for bugs; one weekend Dong visited to find welts on her back the size of a two-yuan coin. After that Dong's mother tried living with them, but the city didn't suit her, and she fought with Dong all the time, complaining about the mother-in-law who showed her face once after the birth and never came again. Then Dong remembered me: I was the perfect solution. "It'll be just like when we were girls," she exclaimed. She spoke with un-complicated fondness, as one who looks back on a past life, certain it was her own character and ability that delivered her to better shores.

My first week of work, Dong and her husband took me out to dinner at a nice restaurant where they ordered a whole fish. After-ward we walked through the bustling night streets, observing the street hawkers and their wares and every once in a while ducking into the humming cool of an air-conditioned shop. "Isn't this incredible, this feeling?" Dong said, turning back to smile at Guagua, who sat alert in my arms, and though I knew exactly what she meant—this feeling that the world was big and colorful and buzzing out of its boundaries—I said nothing. "I'm so pleased you can share in my life," she said. She tried on a few pairs of shoes, high-heeled designs made of real ox skin, and asked me which pair I liked best. "How should I know?" I said. "They all look the same to me." Her husband paid without looking at the price. The next morning, I found the box beside my cot with a note: *For Xia*. The shoes were impossible to stand in. They looked ridiculous with my clothes. I left them in the box, and some weeks later, Dong began to wear them herself.

In those first weeks Dong spoke often of my appearance, commenting on the plainness of my dress or the old-fashioned print of my blouse, how my face shape would be flattered by such and such haircut, offering her lipsticks and brow pens for me to use. I was baffled by this attention; I spent most of my days indoors, covered in her baby's spit. Only later, when I began to see X, did I understand the subtext behind her words. I was twenty-two, single, by some standards on my way to being an old maid. "It must be hard to find a man you like in the village," Dong said knowingly. "We've known them all since they were boys." Some weekends when I returned home, my mother asked me, with much suggestion, if I'd met anyone interesting. "Oh yes," I said, laughing, "the rich city men can't resist a woman with a baby attached to her hip."

Eventually I *did* help myself to Dong's lipsticks and brow pens. I helped myself to her closet, to her modern-cut dresses that suited my figure better than hers, everything except the shoes she'd pretended to buy for me. I spent hours in front of her mirror, looking at my face from various angles, trying to make myself pretty. People change when they're in love: this was something I'd known, from songs and stories. But I didn't really know it until it happened to me.

GUAGUA WAS A TYRANT ON the train ride back. She refused to sleep though it was her nap time, and insisted that I devote every fiber of my attention to her. If I even looked out the window, she would start growling, a playful growl that I knew could mount quickly into a guttural scream. This was something I liked about Guagua. She didn't cry, instead when she wanted my attention she shouted, not inconsolably or in desolation but almost joyfully, like a Taiwanese rock musician hollering into a microphone. I sat her on my lap, facing me, singing songs, talking nonsense, tapping her nose and ears and mouth. Her mother was always telling me that I should be teaching her things, how to count or even to read, it was never too early—Dong, I was discovering more and more, was a truly unreasonable woman—but Guagua would not have it, she grabbed my finger and chewed on it, she attacked my face and neck and hair, she slobbered all over the beautiful red blouse X had unbuttoned just hours before.

I adored her—I really did. She was not mine, but she was so small, and charming in her smallness and fatness, and though she was useless she declared her needs clearly, without suggestion or subtext. I wanted to despise her; sometimes, when she exhausted or disgusted me, I wanted to despise her very much. But it was impossible.

When Guagua was very small, the first day I had been alone with her, she had cried and cried and cried. She was not yet four months old. I was going mad. I put my finger in her mouth and for a moment was relieved: silence. But within a breath she spat my finger out and began to cry even louder than before. I remember pacing the room, alternately carrying her and setting her down, clapping my hands over my ears, thinking that this job would kill me, wondering why no one had warned me that the arrival of a child was no joyous thing but a sort of curse, wondering why all my life people had spoken of marrying and having children like the ultimate blessing. I would never have children, I thought, not if I could help it, and at that moment I put my hands into my pockets and found, as if by a miracle, a hard candy wrapped in a little paper.

I unwrapped the candy and held it in the baby's mouth. For a full minute she sucked at it contentedly, with what I even imagined was a little smile. Now that she had stopped crying she was looking at me languorously. What sort of magical creature was this, she might have been wondering, who possessed such a sugary breast? Her little lips lapped at the edges of my fingers, which were still holding on to the shrinking sweet, and then the candy slipped through them, into her mouth, and down her throat.

My breath stopped. I cupped her face and looked into it— wide-eyed, red, pupils black and piercing—sure that I had killed her. "Please," I said, and it was the first time in my life I'd found myself in a state resembling prayer. "Don't die," I begged her, squeezing her hot little face, and she gulped, and opened her mouth, and laughed.

What a strange elation washed over me then. I felt we had entered into a secret contract, Guagua and I. When she cried later, I did not take it personally, I would laugh at her, saying, "Don't pretend to be unhappy, I know you like me, you stayed alive for me," and in this way, she became an easy child.

But she was not easy that day after we left X's apartment. Even when we returned to Dong's, she would not quiet for a nap. Her rambunctiousness grew an edge and she prowled around the room knocking things over. She pulled on the folded blankets and they fell over her head, enveloping her, and she began to holler, not stopping even when I extracted her. She flailed her tiny arms and legs with a new strength she did not know, striking me, hollering all the while, and I lay down on my back and held her in the air at arm's length, hollering back at her until she grew confused and stopped. But she was still annoyed, her tiny brow furrowed in frustration. She swiped at me and grabbed my cheek and squeezed, hard. "OW!" I said, out loud. I forgot she was a child and I an adult. I grabbed her cheek and squeezed it back, hard.

Her face contorted, as if in slow motion, her mouth turning down and pulling wide, her eyes squinting, her cheeks wrinkling, and she began to sob, genuinely, heartbroken, with a look of utter betrayal. "Well," I said, pulling her to my chest and patting her back, "whose fault is this?" then, with a softened voice: "Calm down, I still like you. I forgive you for hurting me, okay?" I shushed her gently, trying to make my voice loving and sweet, but I failed to calm her. Instead her heartbreak infected me, and I began to sob too. Clutching Guagua to my chest, I rocked back and forth, unable to soothe myself, not knowing what I was crying for, the sobs issuing from my throat like some poison my body needed to expel. When I finally exhausted my sorrow, parched and still, I saw that Guagua had quieted too. Her little nose was crusted with snot, and her pink mouth fell open, whistling in sleep.

I WAS AGITATED THAT WEEKEND. My mother could not stand to look at me. "Go do something useful," she said, and so I picked up the shovel and went up the path to weed the spring crop. It was a bright afternoon. The wind blew benevolently, and in its breath the tender bamboo bobbed their heads in gentle agreement. Beside the path the creek babbled clear and fast—high up in the mountains, the icicles were just now melting in the caves—and on its banks little purple wildflowers poked out their sweet mouths as if waiting to be kissed. My hometown could be effortlessly magnificent, whether with the caressing tenderness of spring or the bleak terror of winter. Sometimes I let myself be rocked by this lie.

Not today. I trampled the path, kicking up bits of mud to spray in those purple petal faces. "Now that I live in the city," Dong had said last week—it was how many of her declarations began—"I can finally appreciate the beauty of the village. When I was a child I saw only poverty, but now I'm amazed by the lushness. Maybe we should bring Guagua to the countryside, just once in a while, to breathe the fresh mountain air." The beauty of the country, I'd thought, what stupidity.

I was walking like this, a brute, when on the opposite bank of the creek I saw the face that wiped every trace of comprehensible thought from me: X. I blinked: it was still him. He was not alone. Beside him walked another person, a person I had never seen before, a woman.

She was his height, gangly and large, boxy around the shoulders. She wore a brown suit with large shoulder pads and a shin-length skirt, the kind of outfit made to be a cheap imitation of something Dong might wear. On her feet were the most insensible shoes, shiny red high heels that looked more whorish than elegant, which sank into the mud every other step, causing her to walk like a mantis, with slightly bent knees. Yet she walked ably, plucking the heels out without much ado, unaware of or indifferent to how ridiculous she looked. She wore her awkwardness as the only option known to her, so her plainness presented itself with a strangely wholesome grace.

For some moments I stood stock-still, watching this woman and X. I watched and considered whether I should allow X to see me—in muddy field clothes, hair awry—until I realized it did not matter, every cell in me wanted, desperately, to be as near to him as I could be. And he was walking toward me, with this woman, the path ended on their side of the creek and they were crossing the stone bridge to where I stood gaping.

I took a long breath of the fresh mountain air. I tried to slow my brain, to control it. I tried to make myself the way I knew a woman should be: mysterious, alluring, secretly maneuvering everything. So I tossed aside the shovel and walked up to X. I didn't say hello. I said, "And where is your jiejie visiting from?" though I knew he had no older sister.

X was surprised. He avoided my gaze, searching for an answer anywhere but in my face. "This is Jinghu," he finally said, gesturing at the woman. Jinghu did not blush, did not register his embarrassment or mine. Face-to-face, I could see she was not just plain but ugly, with a long, severe face and a chin as thick as a man's.

"We're engaged to be married," Jinghu said, completely without humor. "We invite you to the feast in May."

She turned to X and resumed their conversation, stepping past me. She spoke stiffly: "At core, I am a pragmatist. I am competent in a wife's duties, but with an income twice yours, it is sensible that I continue in my job, at least until we have a child. Chairman Mao said, 'Enable every woman who can work to take her place on the labor front.' I believe this arrangement is patriotic as well . . ."

I STOMPED INTO THE HOUSE that evening, threw the shovel in a corner, and propped my muddy boots up on a chair. "What's all this," my mother said, coming out from behind the stove.

She looked at me with distaste, eyebrows narrowing, and began: "This attitude of yours, it's truly unbearable . . ." and so on it went, the insults and demeanments I'd heard all my life, how I was born lazy, hating work, how since I was a child I'd openly sought pleasure and play and comfort, how insufferable it was the way I walked around like I deserved something, but who did I think I was, a nobody who didn't even finish primary school, it was no wonder I still had no match, who would want to marry a woman like me, who acted like some kind of royal beauty but was really nothing but a dirty balled-up rag. I snapped back at my mother with sharp words so practiced I did not hear what they were. I didn't say what I was really thinking—*But you were happy, weren't you, when I dropped out of school, you praised me, you wanted more hands in the fields*—it was too true to be ammunition. From the corner where my father sat listening to the old radio came his habitual cough, choked with phlegm. "That's enough," he said in his cracked voice. "Lay off her, you're being harsh," he said to my mother, then to me, sternly: "You should treat your mother with respect. She has a point. It's about time you stopped acting like a child and contributed to this family."

I jumped up, livid. "Don't I, don't I?" I said, souring my face. I dug out the cash Dong had paid me on Friday and threw it on the table, every single bill. I had no use for extra train fare anymore. I ran from the house and wept.

BY THE TIME I BOARDED the bus early Monday morning, the horror of my encounter with X had settled into a hard little lump behind the lungs. My mood cast a damp meaninglessness over everything, draining the passing landscape of color and energy. But if I wanted, I could turn my attention back to that lump and jolt myself into feeling. Instantly, tears sprang to my face, and the pain was so sharp and open it felt indulgent, like licking a bitter, dark sweet.

As the bus wound up and down the mountains, slapping the dew-soaked branches of ferns growing from the cliff, as the sky lightened to dawn, I tended to my self-pity. My mother was right, why would anyone want me, I was stupid and worthless and ugly. X never loved me, never could have loved me, he saw me only as a little sister, a girl to be pitied. But he had kissed me—or had he? My memory swirled in confusion. Perhaps it was I who had kissed him first, or invited it at least, yes, there must have been something in me that was whorish and begging. I replayed the boxy woman's words—*We're engaged to be married*—until they sank with stone finality, replayed them still until they lifted again into bewilderment, then flailing heartache, then anger. I tried to conjure X's face the last time I had seen him in Shanghe, the way he had looked at me, I held on to this image and told myself: He'll never look at you like that again. I twisted the blade. I imagined X turning to the woman in the brown suit with that same look, offering his arms, his kisses, the warmth of his attention. Then X was on his knees, crawling back to me, begging forgiveness. He was renouncing his family, his job, his life, promising me everything in return. I would respond with cold silence, he'd follow me around like a little dog. For days, for months—how long would I let him suffer before I offered him a word? But no—I would have no such choice, X was engaged to be married to someone else.

The bus arrived at Shanghe. My breath caught in my throat. I stepped off. I closed my feelings inside the lump. I boarded the shuttle to the train station and sat staring at the back of the seat. At the station I told myself to walk straight to the platform, to disengage my peripheral vision; I would not see X.

But I did see him. Loose-eyed, groomed, in front of the breakfast vendor. He was holding two bags of doujiang and a bag of buns, scanning the station, and the sight of him was so stunning that for a moment I forgot everything and was filled with pure delight, as if in renunciation my imagination had killed him and now he was back from the dead. On his face was the flitting grin, the look of love.

"Doujiang with a block of ice sugar," he said, "and pork buns with sour mustard. Your favorite." He put his arm around me, he kissed me on the cheek. Did my body stiffen? A part of me wanted to turn and run, so sure was I that it was a trick, that I would look down and instead of breakfast he would be holding a long silver knife. "Will you come today to see me? Or if today isn't possible, we'll meet tomorrow like we planned."

I pulled away and continued toward the platform. He followed, tugging me to him, chatting easily as if I had not met his fiancée in the village just two days before. We walked and I wondered if I had invented the village encounter, if my suffering had been self-inflicted, some sick product of a sick mind that took pleasure in its own pain. At the platform I shook myself from his embrace. He offered me a bun and I stared.

"How can you act like this?" I finally said.

His ease dropped; panic filled its place. "It's a huge misunderstanding, please, you have to let me explain." He grabbed my elbow. "Come back today, please. I'll make it up to you, I'll—"

"I can't come back today." I summoned my coldest voice.

"Then tomorrow."

"Not tomorrow either."

"Please, I'll do anything."

I laughed. "I don't have spending money this week. Some people have families to take care of."

"I'll come to you," he said. "I'll take the day off—I'll see your work for a change."

"So that's what you're interested in?" The train was arriving. I went resolutely into the cloud of smoke and strangers, shouting in spite of myself, "That's why you're pursuing me, to get close to Dong?"

"What?" He grabbed me by the shoulders, held me in place. "What are you talking about?" He took something from his pocket. "Look, I found this at home over the weekend."

It was a faded photograph of what looked like the old village schoolhouse. In front of the building, which had been freshly painted, children in uniforms lined up in three neat rows and stared unsmiling at the camera.

"Look—I'm standing right behind you. I remember that day clearly. I was thrilled to be so close to you. Did you know, even then, I loved you, I felt you were different from the others?"

I stared at the photograph, blinking, confused, as the train doors opened.

"Shall I come to you?" X said.

I swallowed. I imagined X in Dong's house, admiring her furniture, discovering that all the clothes I wore were hers.

"No. I'll come."

He pushed the bags of doujiang and buns into my hands. "Here." He tucked the photograph into my purse along with a five-yuan bill. "I love you," he said. Before I boarded, he pulled me to him and kissed me. "You must know I do."

ON THE TRAIN, I WAS all feeling. I examined the memory of his lips on mine. Foreign, like it had happened to someone else. I found a seat, though it was crowded. I poked a straw into the doujiang and drank, and it was sweet.

THE PHOTOGRAPH HAD BEEN TAKEN in 1978, the year before I dropped out. I was in the third grade, Dong and X in fifth. There were thirty students in the school, and we all studied together in the same cramped room with a square-footed woman we called Teacher Hu, who had come to the village from some cold city in the north.

Did X really think I was special? I did not know that I'd existed to him as anything more than one of many younger kids who scattered in the schoolyard when he appeared, sure-shouldered and grand. It was I who thought him special, who, along with Dong and a group of girls, spent hours huddled after school debating the relative merits of X and his rival, Wang, a tall, bespectacled boy who was the top student and teacher's pet. X was the class clown. He talked back to the teacher, played pranks during lessons, and almost always neglected to do his homework. And yet when Teacher Hu scolded him, she seemed to do so with amusement peeking out behind her stern frown, so that at times we felt that in fact X was her favorite student after all. Though his marks were not nearly as good as Wang's or even Dong's, he was not a bad student either, and when he made fun, it was always with a *spirit* of fun—he was never malicious. Only a few times did he go too far, meriting the punishment of the meter stick, and on those occasions, he could be spied after school standing with the teacher, issuing a genuine apology, his head hung not with shame but with sympathy. The next day, the teacher treated him tenderly, as if he were her own son.

Sometime that year, Dong and I agreed that she loved Wang and I loved X. Dong was the one who realized we could not both love one boy. "We must decide," she had said in the prim Mandarin of the radio announcers, "whom we will marry. After all, we can't have the same husband." I nodded. "Which do you want?" she said, looking at me with narrowed eyes, until I said, "You're older, you choose first." For some moments Dong stared into the distance, furrowing her brow as she waded through some precise mental calculus. "I'll have Wang," she said finally, and I said, "Okay," perhaps too brightly and quickly, because I saw the furrow return to her face, the fear that she had chosen wrong.

I replaced my relief with resigned disappointment. "Oh well," I said before she could speak. "Your husband is the better one, but I don't mind, you're older after all."

Dong made a treacly smile: "Your husband is very nice too."

Where was Wang now? We had long ago lost track of him. He had tested into a special high school in the province capital and hadn't returned to the village since. But Dong had ended up marrying a man not unlike him: tall, bespectacled, successful in the most boring way.

Future husbands became our favorite game. We fantasized about them, about our future lives. Dong said she and Wang would live in a two-story house with concrete walls, that I'd live down the way in a one-story house that was a little smaller but also made of concrete (when she was feeling generous, she gave me a big courtyard). She said she would have three children, two boys and one girl, and I said I'd have the same. We speculated on the favorite foods and pastimes of our future husbands, on whether they'd be silent after dinner or talkative, whether they'd be spoiling fathers or disciplinarians, if their feet would smell after a long day out working.

In secret I had other fantasies, which were so sweet I did not even want to tell Dong, afraid that their power would dissipate the moment I shared them. None of them involved a house in the village or cooking dinner or children. They took place somewhere I could not articulate or even fully imagine, a place at once hazy and bright, a realm of pure feeling. Perhaps it was this secret dream that eventually pushed Dong to act in the ways she did. I deferred to her, openly declared myself her follower, I admired her incessantly and let her treat me as a slave. But it was not enough.

She sensed that I possessed something wonderful, that this thing had nothing to do with her, in fact made me not need her. Without knowing what it was, she wanted to take it away.

HIS PARENTS HAD MADE THE match, X told me that afternoon. It had been arranged for a long time, for so long in fact that he had ceased to believe it was anything more than a childhood story until she appeared in the flesh that afternoon. Not only was she hideous, he said, she was soulless, to speak with her was to be hit in the head dully by the dreariest textbook. We were sitting on the floor of his room and he was talking fast. Now and then he touched me: on the shoulder, on the arm, on the knee.

Guagua was in a state of pure pleasure. She made faces at X, cooing and ahhing like she had fallen in love. He poked at her face and she grabbed his finger. She laughed her sweet little laugh. It was impossible not to fall in love with her too. X picked her up and sat her on his lap. She grabbed his pinkie fingers and waved his arms around.

"Ask me anything," he said. "I'll tell the truth."

"Do you love her?"

"Of course not."

"Do you kiss her?"

"To kiss her would be like kissing a cabinet with feet."

"Will you marry her?"

"I will do everything in my power to prevent it."

"Do you love me?"

"More than anything."

"What would you do for me?"

"I would die."

I did not ask if he would marry me.

The knowledge was already sinking. He would marry the woman automaton. It was a good match and he would fulfill it, taking, as we all would, the path of least resistance.

The hour approached for him to return to work and for me to return to the city. I stood slowly, heavy with my new understanding. X walked me to the train station. We waited on the platform for the second time that day, like stutters of ourselves. He told me again how he loved me.

I looked down the snaking track for the train. Weeds poked up through the slabs of the tracks, their heads singed and flowering. I opened my mouth and closed it. "You really loved me when we were children?" I finally said.

"Yes."

"Did you know—did you know I loved you too?"

"Really?" He shook his head.

"So you don't remember," I said, "a time in the fifth grade, the year that photograph was taken, when Dong told you about my feelings?"

It had been Dong's idea. She had said it was necessary: to ascertain we'd chosen husbands correctly, we had to confess. I had not wanted to. "Are you afraid?" she'd asked. With a tone of benevolence, she proposed to tell X for me. If he loved me back, she would tell me, and if not, I would be spared the shame.

"That never happened."

"You're a liar."

X picked up my hand and dropped it. The train came barreling in, spewing hot wind in our faces.

"Once Dong came to me," X said, shouting over the engine, "to tell me *she* loved me. I only remember it because I thought she was such a snob. I don't think I was very nice." When I didn't respond, he said, "Look at me. I never loved Dong. I never even liked her. She acted like she was better than everyone else. It was always you I loved."

He passed me Guagua, who gave a squawk of discontent, contorting her body back toward X. "Come back tomorrow?" he said, adding, "Like we planned?" And then the train was pulling away, and I was somehow standing on it, gripping Guagua so hard she grumbled and began to scream.

LATE THAT NIGHT, AFTER I put Guagua to sleep, I looked at X's photograph. The girls stood in a line, sullen-cheeked with short-cropped hair, all wearing the same drab school clothes. If X had not pointed me out, I might not have seen myself. But there I was, wearing an expression I did not remember possessing, something between defiance and boredom, standing in front of his younger self.

The boy X—he was the image I had searched for, in my visits to Shanghe, in my return to his apartment, in my readiness to board a train to wherever. The fading memory of this boy, his mouth twitching into a grin, his body readied like an arrow. And the moment he let go—the flight—was that the feeling I pressed for when I kissed him? Even if I hadn't possessed it, the purity of this imagined flight, nurtured in the privacy of my lone self, was the closest to freedom I'd reached. That was why I had not wanted Dong to tell X of my love, not that I was afraid or ashamed. I'd wanted to keep it mine.

I found Dong at the other end of the row. She looked remarkably as she did now.

The confession had taken place after school, on a humid fall day. I left for home while Dong confronted X in the schoolyard. I remember running back to the village, bare feet slapping the hot, hard dirt all the way to Dong's doorstep, where I sat waiting, heart racing, for her return. When she appeared, her face was twisted with genuine remorse. Somehow, I remembered this clearly, she had managed it so that a single tear was rolling down her face. Before she spoke, I resigned myself. No matter what she said, I had lost him. But what she did say twisted me further. She explained, in painstaking detail, how excited he had been at first when she approached him. How his face had fallen. How he'd said, "It's a pity, I could never love Xia, because I'm in love with you."

"Of course I rejected him," Dong had said, taking my hand. "You're my best friend." She was shaking a little. She held me and we cried together.

That night, I fell ill. The next day I stayed home from school. The day after that I was still unwell, and the day after that I told my mother I didn't want to go to school anymore. She said, "Fine, do what you like," and I never went again.

I turned out the light and lay down beside Guagua, wide awake. The sweetness had drained from my suffering. What had earlier been an alive and flailing pain had hardened into stone. I twisted the knobs that might move me: I thought again of young X and young Dong, I thought of the woman in the brown suit. Just a little scooping, but there was not much to gather. In the next room I could hear the muffled sounds of Dong with her husband, their awkward groans of exaggerated passion, and if there had been anything left inside me, even a bite of bitterness, I would have laughed out loud.

"Like we planned," X had said as I was leaving the station. I knew what he'd meant. I was to meet him alone, so we could make love. Through the muddle I now saw the unnecessary euphemism that had shrouded our previous encounters, how he had given gifts and money and sweet words for one objective, which was clear as day. I wanted to laugh now, to tell him, I've never felt cheap for wanting you. I turned over the stones inside me and saw:

I still did not feel cheap for wanting X.

I still wanted X.

I could devote my sleeplessness to these questions—whether to go tomorrow, whether to believe him, what would become of me—I could torture myself over them all night long, but there would be only one outcome. I slept, I dreamt of flight.

I WOKE EARLY THE NEXT morning surrounded by bright light, the proximity of a self I'd grieved and given up. I lay awake with my eyes closed and let her return to me. I moved through the feelings that were mine again and ate them up. The anticipation of seeing X. The open want that accompanied the image of his face, his hands. The impatience filling my body. The fist of desire clenching and releasing in the most delicious part of me. The pleasure of knowing my want—the pleasure of knowing I would fulfill it.

I sat up and looked at Guagua. It was five thirty and she would wake soon, babbling for her first meal. I fixed a bottle of powdered milk and nudged it into her mouth. For some moments she sucked on it contentedly in dream, then her eyes wedged open and she looked sleepily at me. When she was done, she pushed away the bottle and we lay there staring at each other. It was unnerving, the way she watched me, blinking slowly. She began to crawl to me, over me, little hands grabbing at my hair and neck and arms, washing me in her milk scent. Normally I would have shushed her back to sleep but today I let her play, I made faces and shapes with my hands, drawing her into wakefulness. I changed her diaper. I put her on the floor with a few toys and let her crawl around the room while I started a pot of porridge. Dong and her husband got up, ate, prepared to leave for work.

Guagua did not normally see her mother in the mornings and so began to cry, crawling to Dong and then back to me. Dong picked her up and tried to comfort her, petting her head like a girl playing with a doll. Guagua screamed louder. Dong tickled her feet. "Give her to me, she hates that," I said, and took the baby outside for a walk. When we returned, Dong was gone.

It was around the time Guagua would normally have woken for her second meal of the morning. I fed her, but lightly; I did not want her to fall back asleep, not until I was ready to leave. We continued to play. Guagua grew delirious. I had gambled that with her temperament, this would translate into not fussiness but a toddling exuberance, and I was right. She moved about wildly and without coordination, and in her state a new laugh came out, something between a cackle and a bark. She kissed me wetly on the face, she blew raspberries into my chest, she found my thumbs and put them in her mouth and screamed with delight. Oh how I loved her then, the sweet wild thing! She was made of something both her parents had lost long ago, and I saw suddenly that she was her own person, wholly so, it mattered not a bit who had made her, I would love her completely for all my life.

Sometime in the night, the image of boy X had left the photograph and entered me. As I played with Guagua, as I mirrored her wildness, falling into her rapturous joy, this boy emerged, golden and running in the sun. Not the memory of X exactly, but his echo—a boy in the image of X. I could make him, I realized, I could keep him for myself. I could create his freedom, tend to it, and protect it, perhaps even have it for a while. My want was alive, kicking its legs. I hugged Guagua and I was hugging my own boy. She laughed and it was his laugh. I cradled her and was nursing him.

I dressed quickly. I knew what I wanted to wear, a white suit that had never appealed to me before; on Dong it looked too professional and stiff. I stepped into the shoes she had bought for me, accepting her apology. The square shoulders of the jacket and long lines of the legs did not make me severe. Rather, my beauty looked effortless. My hair shone, falling across my face sensuously; even without lipstick my lips were red and full. I fed Guagua again, stirring formula into porridge, a huge portion. When she was past satiated I took her outside once more, walking slowly, singing her favorite song, a song about mothers and jewels, rubbing her back until her mouth was open in sleep. Miraculously she did not soil my suit. I placed her gently onto the cot.

For a moment I stood there looking at her. Often she slept like this while I cleaned the house, sometimes for three hours straight. Why should this day be any different? If I was lucky—she was exhausted—she might sleep even longer.

I thought for a minute. If she woke, she could roll and crawl—I couldn't leave her on our cot. I took her to her parents' bed. I drew the curtains to make the room dark. I lined the floor around the bed with pillows and blankets. Guagua stirred and I sat next to her, singing softly until she quieted. "I love you, sweet little melon head," I whispered into her ear. I kissed the top of her fuzzy head.

IN THE SECTION BETWEEN TWO train cars I stood, next to an open window. I was light, happy for the jostling floor beneath me, for the dusty wind that whipped and knotted my hair. Without Guagua, my arms seemed to float. I was holding X's photograph, looking idly at the grinning boy. Yes, I thought, this image is already inside me. My eyes moved to Dong. I searched for cunning, for jealousy, for that spark of willfulness that glowed hot and fervent in my memory. But her girl face looked back blankly, betraying only ignorance.

I held the photograph out the window. Our young bodies flapped in the wind. They caught the current and tugged, and I let them fly.

In Shanghe, X stood in his usual place, his posture solemn, almost mournful. It was a hot day and flies buzzed about the platform, making his image swim. In a momentary flash I saw the man who had stood next to his fiancée with his head bowed and nothing much to say. They were suited to each other, the ugly woman with the decent job, the factory boy whose good looks were already turning south.

I stepped off the train and ran to him. I shaped him back into the X that eluded me. "Wow," he said, a little fear in his voice. He took my hand, and a cloud of pleasure enfolded me. He held me by the wrist and led me through Shanghe, through the alleys we had walked with Guagua. In a daze I thought of her. Her little body on her parents' bed, curled in sweet sleep. I saw her hollering—on the floor, bleeding, tangled in blankets, in blankets tangled around her little nose and mouth and throat, blue and unblinking. "Don't die," I whispered to her, "please."

"What?"

We had arrived in his room. X was closing the door, straightening the furniture, moving toward me.

I laughed, a laugh like a cry. I grabbed his arm and pulled him to me. I kissed him. He buried his hands in my hair. He clawed at Dong's buttons and belt and zipper, wedging his hand beneath my panties, he kissed and caressed my neck. "Do you love me?" he said, hot into my ear. I thought of Guagua sleeping peacefully; I thought of the boy inside me, his spindly legs, his mischievous face, his messy hair, running through tall grass. "I love you," I said. He pushed me down and entered me, and I told myself, *Keep this, all of this*, and I did.

With Feeling Heart

Xiaoyi says the way to a good life is to give everything. Give where there is need, she says. Never ask for anything back.

She is spooning rice into a plastic bag. She scoops up a fried egg. She slices a block of luncheon meat.

Do you like sour mustard? she shouts over the balcony.

The man shouts back:

I'm starving, I'll eat anything.

Okay—get ready!

She ties the bag with a double knot and drops it over the ledge. Four floors below, the man waits with arms outstretched. He has long, ragged hair and cracked and mottled skin, the kind of man who would frighten me if I met him on the street. He plunges his nose into the bag, inhaling. I am five. I know one life. In this life adults put up with me because they think that I am good. Which is an absolute: not something I can try to do but something I have, like a talent, I'm either born with it or not.

A woman shouts from across the alley:

Don't bother with him, he's a liar! I just fed him a bowl of mian.

Maybe he's still hungry, Xiaoyi snaps back. Then, to the man: You have a good day, sir. She shuts the balcony door and turns to me:

Mengmeng, a person should not judge another. The feeling heart should be open wide.

She speaks with the gentle drawl I will long associate with wisdom, with compassion, until the years press it into something else. I imagine her voice dressed in monk's robes, its bare feet climbing up the long temple steps.

When I see a hungry man I feed him, the monk voice continues. When I see need, I don't turn away. See, your mother asks me to care for you, to hold you and feed you and wash your clothes, and I do. You may look at my life and think, It's not much. But I'm not in anyone's debt.

Xiaoyi talks about giving and taking, what she has given and what others have taken, and how she has refused repayment, stacking debts twofold. I imagine *good* as an inside-out bank. The more people owe you, the richer you are.

Just look at you, she says. When you grow up, you'll take care of your mother. You'll have no obligation to remember me.

I'll remember you, I protest.

Xiaoyi laughs.

No, shisandian, you'll forget me, just like you've forgotten . . .

She lists relatives: a guma, a jiugong, an ahpo, a yeye whose face I *have* forgotten and must conjure from leftover scraps. He got my mother a visa and me some nice new clothes, Xiaoyi says, and has no grandchildren of his own. I remember one photograph of my mother's departure; I imagine he is the stranger who holds me as I wail in the windy airport lot.

And does your mother write to thank him, Xiaoyi asks, does she call him on the New Year?

She gives an amused smile. I'm not saying you'll be heartless, she says. But trust me, you'll forget.

Outside, the hungry man is singing. Pity, pity, he sings melodiously, pity for a hungry man like me. Singing he walks down the alley and out of my life, a walk I will take soon too. Out of my one life and into America, through the alleys of twenty years and counting, where we finally meet again on the street.

His hair is long and ragged. His skin is mottled and cracked. He is still singing. Singing as he circles the sidewalk in bare and swollen feet, twirling a chef's knife like a wand. Not an uncommon sight in this America, and now in these "unprecedented times." Even my mother, who has seen everything, is now routinely surprised. In these times to cross the street could be read as fear, but also as care for his health and mine. I do not cross. I step into the bike lane, where no one is coming, and look him in the eye. Kindly. "You have a good day, sir," I say.

He stares: his stare closes a vise grip on mine. I have half a mind to leave my backpack of groceries at his feet. Instead I hurry past. I turn a corner and for shame I run. Through streets pitched with tents, past broken needles and shattered glass, past shifting shapes beneath shelters of tarp, I run, past Porsches parked behind Teslas, past dried scabs of excrement, I run. In these times the way I know to soothe myself is to keep imagining. I wipe off the grime and wear, and he is yellow like me. He laughs and pulls out—a fork! A table appears—he sits—then noodles, and a fried egg. He plunges his nose into the bowl, raises his knife—and fork!—laughing. No, it is a prime rib—and I am nearly home. In these times I've grown tired of my heart, how much feeling it has required, and would much prefer to laugh. But there it is, thumping.

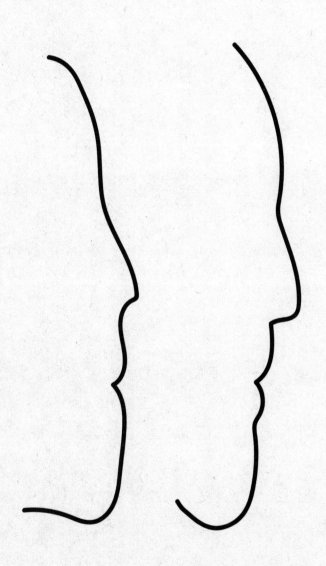

Selena and Ruthie

"Clear and pure," the choral director had said, "like a pour of cold water."

He was talking about Selena's voice. Selena whom he had placed at the top corner of the risers, whose lanky enthusiasm had once or twice nearly teetered her off the edge. He had placed her there so that her clear tone and impeccable pitch might wash over the hooligans he had for a chorus and keep them relatively in tune. His calculation had been spot-on. For a moment he closed his eyes and listened to the group, all singing in Selena's voice. This was the magic of Selena: she was so good she disappeared.

Then Ruthie stepped out, and the spirit flew from her mouth. Ruthie's voice—raw, expressive, a ray of light made visible, beautiful, by flecks of floating dust—in a chorus it stuck out like a sore thumb. The director had placed her front and center in hopes that the many Selenas behind and around her might blend her out. "Save your voice for the solo," he'd told Ruthie. "Mouth the rest if you have to."

Ruthie sang her last brilliant note. She flicked her eyes back to Selena, who gave a bright smile of affirmation, before stepping back into the row. After the concert they linked arms and walked out the flung-open front doors. An unlikely pair: Selena stick thin with short black hair, flat-chested and narrow-hipped like a boy; Ruthie already sporting double Ds, with orange-red curls and those eyes that stared. Selena tall, Ruthie short; Selena shy, Ruthie bold. Selena whom he hadn't noticed until stumbling over her name on the attendance roster—was it Chinese? Japanese? No, their names were longer. "You can call me Selena," the thin voice piped—and he'd been surprised, later delighted, she hadn't signed up for orchestra instead. Ruthie who wore the unmistakable face of her big brother, Samuel, the charismatic troublemaker. Teachers had passed him on to the high school at the end of last year with both regret and relief. Ruthie had Samuel's rebellious streak, yes, but used it mostly to roll her eyes. Ruthie and Selena. The director looked upon their diminishing forms in satisfaction. His star, and the clear night against which she shone.

"CH-CH-CH-CHANGES," RUTHIE SANG IN THE car. Carol's car— Carol was Ruthie's mom—a beige minivan with big soft dents on the doors. The inside was filled with cardboard boxes from whose open tops spilled stacks of CDs and books from the library. Bowie on the stereo, the moth scent of yellowing paper, Ruthie's voice ringing effortlessly from the front: in this habitat Ruthie and Carol resided in Selena's memory, long after she no longer sat in the back seat. Selena crossed her legs over *Crime and Punishment* and hummed along nervously. She didn't know how to sing unless she was *singing*, that is, back straight, diaphragm engaged, mouth shaped into a correctly formed vowel.

"You guys sounded really good," Carol said. "Fucking super, seriously."

Ruthie rolled down the window and belted at the red light.

"Thanks, Carol," Selena said. "Ruthie was *super* on her solo."

Carol was unlike any mom Selena could imagine. She wore baggy band T-shirts and ripped jeans, and her long curtain of thin, dry hair was dyed inky black. She cursed freely and spoke to the girls not exactly as if they were adults but as if the fact that they weren't didn't mean a thing. She took Ruthie to punk rock concerts and paid for things like nose piercings. She insisted Selena call her Carol, not *Ms. Rubin* or "Ruthie's mom," as Selena had done the first time Carol had given her a ride home, after a late rehearsal when Carol saw Selena sitting on the curb alone. The bus had gone and Selena's dad wouldn't be off work for another couple of hours.

"You're a good singer," Ruthie had said when Selena climbed into the van. From then on they were friends, and Carol was their chauffeur.

In Carol's van, Selena visited parts of the city she had never seen: record shops and bookstores and a cafe bakery where she and Ruthie huddled over cheesy soup served in the hollow of a round loaf of bread. Okay, so Selena had moved there the summer before, and knew only the halting, winding path through apartment complexes and trailer parks the school bus took from where she lived to the leafy streets of the middle school. Her chatter-shocked bus of Black and Mexican kids (plus herself) pulled into a busily scooting line of SUVs and vans like Carol's, each emitting one or two kids who looked more or less like Ruthie, but with smaller breasts, duller hair, and fewer piercings. The bus doors sighed open; two cities tentacled into one.

Carol knew everything there was to know, every band worth listening to, every book worth reading, every politician worth hating. In the van, Selena heard for the first time the names and songs of not just David Bowie but Nirvana and Queen and Pearl Jam. She was handed dog-eared novels by Kurt Vonnegut and John Steinbeck and Philip Roth; Carol finished reading a book, deemed it "life changing," and handed it to Ruthie, who read it and passed it to Selena. Selena was amazed. She had not thought of life as something that could be changed, of change as something you could bring upon yourself, something you could want.

"She gets straight As," Selena overheard Ruthie say to Carol once, "but she's never heard of Sylvia Plath?" Ruthie, Selena knew, had not just heard of Sylvia Plath but read every word Sylvia Plath had ever written, yet she got Bs in English and even Cs and Ds in math. Selena knew grades like Cs and Ds existed, but she didn't believe it, not really. Wouldn't you have to *try* to do so badly? Maybe all of Ruthie's brilliance burned straight into her voice, leaving little for the rest of her. Selena possessed a painfully democratic capability—competent at most things but brilliant in none—of which singing was just the latest application.

"She's sheltered," Carol told Ruthie, "and she doesn't think she's too smart to study."

Selena had run back inside to get her algebra textbook. She waited a few moments before knocking on the window with a loud "Hiya!" The previous week Carol had glimpsed her father coming home in his pizza delivery uniform—"Thanks for caring Selena!" he'd said cheerfully before abruptly shutting the door—since then, Carol's look of knowing kindness had grown more pitying. Selena didn't mind being pitied; sometimes she pitied herself too. To Carol's inquiries Selena had replied that her father was a scientist in training at the local university and only delivered pizzas at night. Selena had sampled the wide offerings of the menu from mistaken deliveries and customers' changes of heart, and rattled off her favorites from the back seat: "Thin crust, green pepper, mushrooms, black olives, no onions, ew, oh and the fire chicken wings, they're more sour than spicy, actually. The salads are not very good."

They pulled up to Selena's building. Her unit's window was black.

"Looks like your dad's not home yet," Ruthie said.

Selena jangled her keys; she was doing a silent jig inside. "See you at the audition tomorrow!" she said. "Thanks for the ride, Carol!"

In the cocoon of her empty apartment, Selena dropped her backpack on the dirty brown carpet and bolted the door. She cracked an egg into a pot of instant ramen and ate cross-legged in front of the TV, then took out the sheet music Ruthie had lent her for the spring musical audition. Ruthie had made her sign up for the audition and pinkie swear they'd do it together. Selena sat down at the electric keyboard where she practiced for piano lessons, played the intro, and began to sing—

"I could have daaaaanced all night . . ."

Soon Selena was waltzing across the brown carpet, hairbrush in hand—was it a universal truth that one sang better while gripping a microphone-shaped object?—her voice soaring as it reached the high notes, the glimmer of a budding vibrato ringing through as her breath ran out. In Chorus she was all control, the pleasure of singing near mathematical: figuring the notes on the staff, the pitch and time and dynamic and tone markings, executing them as close to how they were written as she could. But there was nothing quite like singing alone. You opened your mouth and trusted. You forgot who you were. Sometimes, the sound that poured out made you feel like you could be anybody. Selena could hear her smile pull up the corners of her vowels. Her singing sounded different when she was smiling. Did it sound—more like Ruthie's?

There was a banging on the door:

"HOW MANY TIMES—I GOTTA TELL YOU—TURN YOUR GODDAMN MUSIC—"

Jimmy from upstairs drove long-distance trucks overnight and needed to sleep whenever he was home. Jimmy probably had a great singing voice, Selena thought, it boomed and resonated with such force. "Sorry, Jimmy," she said, walking toward the door, "I got carried away . . ." But on the other side, another voice was already apologizing:

"So sorry! *Jimmy*, she is just kid . . ."

"Just sayin', I gotta go *drive*, I gotta be on them roads and I gotta be *awake*—"

"Selena know, I talk her, bring for you pizza one day, okay?"

"Okay, okay, I gotta go, peace, man."

"Peace be to you, Jimmy, and sweet dream."

The lock clicked open. Selena's father was home. Grinning, holding up a bag of fire wings in one hand. "You know the advantage of not having a real piano," he said in Mandarin, "is you can practice with the sound turned off? Try it, maybe you'll develop intuitive muscle memory." He winked. "Or were you singing again? Didn't get enough of that at the concert?"

IN HOMEROOM THE NEXT MORNING, Helen plopped her backpack down next to Selena's.

"So, which Science Olympiad teams are you signing up for?" Helen asked.

"I . . . um . . ." Selena glanced around warily, lowering her voice so Helen might edge closer and lower hers. "Was that supposed to be today?"

"Um, yes."

Helen was the other Chinese girl in sixth grade. Round-faced, glossy-haired, nerdier than Selena but somehow less afraid. Before Ruthie, Helen had been her only friend. Assigned to the same homeroom, they had gravitated toward each other on the first day of school, Selena hesitant, unable to look at Helen straight until Helen blurted out, in a sharp voice that made Selena cringe, "Are you Chinese?" With haste and a touch of relief

Selena said yes. They continued like this, asking the questions that were asked of new friends—favorite color, favorite animal, Doritos Cool Ranch or Nacho Cheese—until they discovered that they both had birthdays in the month of June. "June power, yes!" Helen said, pulling down two fists like she had scored a prize. "June power," Selena repeated, "cool!" Having discovered something other than Chineseness to bond them, she relaxed.

There had always been a seed of embarrassment in Selena's friendship with Helen; and why should it be embarrassing, her father would say, that the only person who'd befriended her was also Chinese? Helen was confident, assertive—perhaps because like Ruthie, she had breasts, though she wore them like she wore her oversized backpack, with a begrudging shrug. A notch short of bossy, Helen spared Selena the anxiety of which clubs to join, where to sit in the cafeteria, whose locker to visit between classes. Next to Ruthie, however, Helen was a child.

Years later, when Selena remembered herself from that time, she would shake her head at her own childness, looking upon the image of her child body with a kind of sad shock. And yet, when she turned her mind's eye to Ruthie, against all cognitive reason it conjured a fully grown woman. It was not just that Ruthie had breasts and excellent posture. Around Ruthie, Selena felt that she was in the presence of somebody who had already become who she was.

"I can't do Science Olympiad, I'm auditioning for the musical," Selena said, raising her voice. "I promised Ruthie I would. Science Olympiad was always your thing anyways."

The bell rang for first period. They slung their backpacks over their shoulders and filed out of the room. Behind Selena, Helen was saying, "But you were so good at birds, you could identify them just by their calls . . ."

Selena was already bounding down the hall.

FIRST PERIOD, SOCIAL STUDIES, WAS the one class besides Chorus she had with Ruthie. Their teacher was a timid white man called Mr. P. They had recently started a unit titled "World Civilizations and Cultures." Last week they had studied "African Culture" and this week they were journeying east. Selena felt nauseous; often she felt nauseous in Social Studies, though she could never put her finger on exactly why.

Last week, Mr. P had read out loud from the textbook: "Much of what we know about African culture comes from the work of archaeologists, as African history is a recent development, arising only in the last two hundred years." This had confused Selena—hadn't they learned that human civilization had *started* in Africa?

"Excuse me!" Chika, who was in seventh grade math with Selena, had waved her hand in the air. "Permission to speak, Mr. P! I think this book has some incorrect information. My family lives in Nigeria and has been there since forever? So, it cannot be correct that African history is only two hundred years old."

"Yeah, didn't we learn that the pyramids was built like five thousand years ago? Ain't Egypt in Africa?" said Jerome. Jerome was the other kid at Selena's bus stop, outgoing and friendly to everyone. Sometimes he talked to Selena until the next stop, chattering easily about nothing and everything, a skill Selena would never have. Then his friends got on and flocked around him, and Selena scooted to the window and put on her headphones to listen to the latest CD Ruthie had burned.

"Nah, Egyptians are white," said Benjamin, who sat next to Jerome, in class and on the bus. On Fridays they huddled together in the back seat, reading comic books Jerome got from his big sister. "Africans are Black, right?"

"*Isn't*," Mr. P corrected. "The pyramids *were* built. Chika. Jerome. Benjamin! Please wait to be called on to speak. Now let's review the definition of *history*. In chapter one, we learned that history is *a written record* . . ."

"What about that—the Rosetta Stone? That was from Africa, right?" said Jerome.

"Yes, the Rosetta Stone was discovered in Egypt," said Chika, "which is in *North* Africa. Not all Africans are Black, Benjamin, you probably just think so because all the ones brought to America with the slave trade were. It's confusing."

"Yo, Mr. P," Benjamin said, "this book is—"

"Enough!" Mr. P had summoned his courage. To show these kids some measure of authority and discipline! He steadied his resolve, he said to himself: *You are the teacher!*

But over the weekend, regret had dogged him. Moments of the class replayed involuntarily, showing him how he might have taught differently. Despite his attempt to assert control, wielding the recognizable signals of power, he had lost a measure of respect. The class had settled, and yet, their eyes had glazed over, their minds had disengaged. What he should have done was so obvious now. He might have invited Chika, who probably did know more about Africa—and why not? She *was* from there—to lead the discussion. At the start of Asia week, he would position himself differently.

"Selena," he said now, kindly, graciously. "Last year Yumei's mom brought in dumplings for the class. Do you think your mother would like to do something like that? She could come in and speak to us about your, erm, cultural traditions . . . ?"

Selena looked up wide-eyed. "I—oh—um—"

"Selena doesn't have a mom, *asshole*," Ruthie said, and was sent to the principal's office for disorderly conduct.

AFTER THE LAST BELL, SELENA ran to the empty chorus room where she was meeting Ruthie to warm up before auditions.

"I can't believe you got in trouble for me!"

"Whatever." Ruthie gestured at the piano. Selena sat.

Selena played scales, nudging their voices up step by step, then down to the notes where Selena's gave way but Ruthie's still sounded, gravelly and rich. In Chorus Ruthie was a mezzo, Selena a soprano. As Ruthie practiced the audition piece, Selena noted that while Ruthie sounded superb as always, there was something missing; she didn't bring out the full potential of the melody, how it allowed you to play with darkness and lightness of tone. Her own voice, malleable, a precisely shaped container into which you could pour any personality, was better suited for the main role. Eliza Doolittle sang brashly in the middle registers before her transformation, but once she became a lady she floated on high Gs like any romantic heroine. Ruthie sounded like herself all the time, not like a person flirting with—on the verge of—transformation.

Selena told Ruthie to sing again. She coached Ruthie. She stopped Ruthie when she was off and told her to repeat. "Open your mouth more, approach the note from the top. Don't *reach* for it, dance on top of it, lightly, like ballet, on tiptoe. It's *night*, but the vowel is *ah*—imagine that you're saying *n-ah-t*. Like that. Much better."

"Now you," Ruthie said when she finished.

Selena took a shallow breath. "I didn't really get a chance to practice."

"Oh, spare me." Ruthie hunted for the starting note on the piano, hit it, and crossed her legs.

Selena began to sing. Selena was singing. Tentative at first— the sound of her voice surprised her each time she heard it, she could not quite believe that it was coming from her. She caressed the sound, she entered the notes. She was emboldened, forgot that Ruthie was watching, and became the words, and the melody that fulfilled their meaning. She sang to the last note, and when it came, she inhaled, shocked, as if doused in cold water.

Ruthie was clapping. Selena blinked and shook herself.

"That was fucking fantastic," Ruthie said. "Dude, I almost cried."

"Just fantastic," said Ms. Clark, the drama teacher, to Selena at the end of her audition. "Where have you been? Oh, sixth grade? A mature voice for your age." Selena walked out beaming. The next day she and Ruthie went to the stage door to check the cast list. Ruthie gripped Selena's hand tight.

"You got the lead!!" Selena said. "I knew it!"

They read down the list of names.

"I don't understand," Ruthie said.

Selena blinked in confusion, not at the absence of her name exactly. At the very bottom of the cast list, under the bolded *Chorus*, where in order to prepare for the worst she had prepared to find her name, she read the words *Helen Li*.

RUTHIE, SELENA, HELEN. SELENA WAS the unhappy glue that held the trio together. She did not like this arrangement, preferring Ruthie and Helen each alone. Or preferring herself when she was with Ruthie or Helen alone. It was not just that they bickered, forcing her to act as mediator. Selena was a different person standing before Ruthie and standing before Helen. To bring the polar aspects of herself together confused and tired her.

Ruthie starred; Ruthie was born to star. Helen sang like a crow and couldn't keep a tune. Selena sewed costumes, painted sets, stripped and dressed Ruthie in quick changes in the wings, inhaling the womanly funk of her sweat. Sometimes Selena winced as she helped Helen practice her part. "What did you even sing for the audition?" she asked Helen meanly, but the answer— "Uh, I don't remember . . . 'Happy Birthday'? I just wanted to see what all the fuss was about!"—just sank her further. She coached Helen and Ruthie both, singing their notes perfectly, insolently, turning a cold ear to Helen's sorry embarrassed incompetence. Sometimes when she helped them rehearse in the auditorium, Ms. Clark would cast her gaze over the three girls, searching for the source of Selena's voice, and stare at Selena, perplexed, before shaking her head and turning away.

Thus the three were initiated to the art of the stage. There was a world of difference between a chorus in *theatre* and a chorus in a concert hall, Selena learned. Whereas in the concert hall you wanted fifty voices to sing as one, in the theatre you hoped five would sound like a hundred or more. You hoped the small dancing and crowing group might evoke the busy chatter of an entire town or city or milieu. Selena came to accept that Helen's casting was no mistake. Selena's voice would have disappeared in that chorus, and she would have been just an extra body onstage. Impossible, besides, that anyone might confuse the two of them, who looked nothing alike.

In future auditions Selena tried to make her voice ugly like Helen's, but it was no use. Ms. Clark had seen Helen perform, with a loping clumsiness that was strangely affecting, and returned to the familiar. Helen added substance and color to the chorus, making it gritty and real, like a face made three-dimensional by shadow. But to have two Chinese girls onstage? Well, *Oklahoma!* wasn't set in Chinatown, was it? And Selena was too wispy, an antimagnet; maybe if your eye traveled in her direction you might notice how expressively and beautifully she sang, but your eye never went to her, period.

In the seventh grade, at a dress rehearsal for *Beauty and the Beast*, Ruthie huddled with Selena and Helen backstage, their faces barely visible in the black-blue light. On the other side of the curtain Gaston was singing with the trio of silly girls, the music stopping and starting as the actor, Julian, forgot his lines. Selena was holding a footstool, which she was supposed to whisk onstage at the end of the song.

"So I just wanted to tell you," Ruthie whispered, uncharacteristically nervous. "I'm bi."

"Bi like bi*sexual*?" Helen said.

"Yup," Ruthie said. "I'm bisexual. Yeah."

"Cool," Selena said.

"Don't you have a boyfriend?" Helen said.

"Um, that's the point? She goes both ways?" Selena said.

The spotlight dimmed: Selena's cue. Light-footed, she pranced on in the dark and set the stool down on the blue tape marking. Ruthie followed and sat on the stool, squeezed Selena's hand before she ran off. The spotlight rose on Ruthie, and her red hair lit up the auditorium.

Watching Ruthie, Selena considered questions that had never occurred to her: Was *she* bi? Was she straight? She was probably not a lesbian, she thought, because she had a crush on a boy—Julian, to be exact: dark-haired, yellow-eyed, ethnically ambiguous Julian who was presently pursuing Ruthie across the stage. He had the voice of an angel. But Selena did think girls pretty; in the locker room before and after PE she had to try not to stare. Was thinking a girl pretty the same as *liking* her? Selena had never kissed anyone, and the thought of it, her lips meeting another set, was equal parts disgusting and exciting. Were the lips attached to a boy or a girl? Selena made a face. She couldn't make it past the lips.

Ruthie, on the other hand, had kissed many lips. On the stage alone—Selena had seen it. Ruthie danced as Julian sang of his love. Did she like kissing? Selena wondered. Julian reached for Ruthie and as she spun away his hand brushed her breast. Maybe once you had breasts you started wanting to kiss people too.

Selena turned to Helen. "Who would you rather kiss?" she said, nodding at the stage.

Helen turned red. "Gross! Neither!"

"Don't you want a boyfriend?"

"Not really."

"If Julian asked you out tomorrow, you wouldn't say yes?"

"Of course not!" Helen crossed her arms. "I would never do that to you."

Suddenly Selena wanted to hug Helen. Ruthie gave hugs without thinking; her body moved in freedom.

"You're a good friend," Selena said, and stroked Helen's arm awkwardly.

THERE WAS MORE OF RUTHIE'S life that Selena longed to enter. She didn't need to be an active participant. She would be content to sit in the wings, in the darkened auditorium, in the back seat in her invisible Selena cloak. For instance, Selena had never even met Ruthie's mythical brother, Samuel. In her mind's eye she conjured how Ruthie might look as a boy. Selena fantasized that Samuel would meet her and see his one true love. Samuel was a bad boy, Selena knew from the way people talked about him, though she didn't know exactly what this meant. Did he have piercings, blue hair, did he smoke? In her fantasies, Selena was the good girl who turned him to the true and lighted path.

Always Ruthie was on the verge of waltzing out, leaving Selena behind. Besides theatre and Chorus and once at Ruthie's

bat mitzvah—everyone agreed she sang the Torah gorgeously—
they did not actually "hang out." Selena did homework. Selena
practiced piano—electric keyboard. In her empty apartment,
Selena made herself ramen noodles and called Helen Li. She sat
on the floor with the receiver pressed against her ear, talking
about nothing. Meanwhile, Ruthie went to the movies with her
boyfriend. Ruthie went to Weezer concerts with her boyfriend.
Ruthie went on double dates with her boyfriend and Samuel and
his girlfriend; one day, Selena dreamed, it would be she across
the table from Ruthie and Samuel. Ruthie's newest boyfriend had
a license and a car; they drove to empty parking lots and made
out. Selena understood that making out was a sort of prolonged
kissing that possibly involved hands. Ruthie's boyfriends were
high school boys, usually friends of Samuel's.

"When will Ruthie go out with a girl?" Selena wondered to
Helen.

"Ruthie, Ruthie," Helen said, and Selena could hear her rolling
her eyes.

"Julian said hi to me today," Selena said with a sigh. "He picked
up my pencil in Spanish."

"Qué amor," Helen said. "But seriously, Julian is probably
gay."

"You think everyone is gay. He could be bi?"

"You think everyone is bi."

On the first day of eighth grade, at lunch, Ruthie was nowhere to be found. Finally Selena saw her outside, sitting on the
bleachers beside the blacktop, huddled in intimate conversation
with a girl Selena knew, kind of. Mousy-faced, brown-haired,
stocky and boyish, with small but present breasts and acne scars
cratering her cheeks. Her name was Michelle, or Michaela.
Selena had seen her around, hanging with the bad kids. Selena
did not consider herself pretty—if she were pretty she would

be popular—but she thought she was probably prettier than Michelle/Michaela.

"So who was that?" Selena asked Ruthie before Chorus. "You were with her at lunch?"

Ruthie's eyes hooded over. "Michelle's having a hard time." She took her seat. "Samuel's a fucking jerk. The narcissistic prick broke up with her, again."

"*She's* Samuel's girlfriend?"

"Well, not currently."

The chord for warm-ups sounded. Selena found her way to the back row. Ruthie's words had opened a gate and peripheral knowledge of Michelle was flooding in, snatches of conversation Selena had not even known she'd caught: . . . *I heard she . . . third base behind the gym . . . 'cause she puts out.* What did Michelle put out and what did it have to do with baseball? Then came a memory of waiting outside the locker room to change for PE. She and Helen were sitting on the bench at the edge of the popular girls' gossip. She'd felt a pinch of exhilaration to be within the bubble of hearing, almost as if they were talking to her. She'd turned to Chika on her other side and whispered, "What's a *hor*?" Chika's bright laugh clanked into her ear. "Selena, you are such a prude." Chika lowered her voice: "A whore is the same thing as a slut."

"Earth to Selena!" The piano had stopped and the director was waving at her. "Are you with us? You're flat! *Ff-lat.* Okay. Start again. And a three and four—"

"IT BARELY HURTS, SEE?"

Michelle had a kind smile and kind eyes. Selena was surprised by the way she spoke, frankly and without affect, like Ruthie but with more . . . hope? Despite the harshness of her looks—

the frayed brown hair, the ink-black eyeliner, the rough, scarred skin—she radiated softness; Selena wanted to curl up against her like a cat. Michelle had carved *SAMUEL* into her left forearm and was pressing into the lip of the thin *S*.

"If you use a sharp enough razor you can't feel a thing. Afterwards it stings a little, but it's a nice pain. Like love."

Selena winced. On Michelle's right arm she saw a ragged web of knotted skin, scars from previous experiments with duller blades.

"My brother is not worth all this," said Ruthie.

Michelle looked away. "I love him," she said.

At home, Selena opened the drawers in the bathroom. Toothpaste, toothbrush, empty, empty, Irish Spring soap. Finally she found the blue plastic razor her father used to shave the wisps of his barely-mustache. She inspected it, tried to pry out a blade. "Ouch!" A clean slice on her thumb, like a large paper cut. The line was white. Selena watched as it filled with bright blood. It stung, yes.

Was this what love felt like? She thought about Samuel, about wanting him and not having him. Yes, the feelings matched: a minor throbbing, dull with little spokes of sharpness. A drop fell and reddened the sink. Selena felt faint. She turned on the water and ran her thumb under it, watching the pink water swirl down the drain until her skin was white and puckered. She bandaged herself up.

The next day Michelle glowed.

"He was moved," she said. "He had tears in his eyes. He loves me too."

A week later, at lunch, Michelle held a lighter to the point of a safety pin. "It's totally sanitized, just like piercing your ears."

Selena rubbed her smooth unpunctured lobes. Michelle brought the pin to the flesh of her own upper arm.

"I cannot," Ruthie said, and turned away.

Selena stared. Michelle wedged the safety pin into her flesh, a millimeter or two deep, twisting it until the sharp point emerged an inch away, and tucked the point into its metal pocket. A bead of sweat rolled off the soft down between her cheek and ear. She let out a huff of air. "There." She smiled.

Two weeks later, Ruthie grabbed Selena's elbow outside Social Studies, which they still had together, first period with Mr. P, as if stuck in some hellish loop.

"We have to talk," Ruthie said. "Michelle slit her wrists. She said it was an accident but—I'm going to fucking kill my brother."

"Ohmygod, ohmygod!" Before she could process the words, Selena was weeping, blubbering a word soup: "Is she okay how horrible *horrible* ohmygod what do we *do*?"

"Jesus." Ruthie wiped Selena's eyes with the sleeve of her shirt. "Get yourself *together*."

Ruthie looked like she could hit someone: Selena, if she didn't stop crying. Selena puckered; she apologized as the bell rang. "Tardy!" Mr. P hollered from inside. They entered to staring eyes.

Mr. P clapped his hands.

"Today, we travel to *Me-ji-co*," he said, "forrrrr *dee-a day las mor-toes*!"

SELENA HAD NEVER BEEN TO a sleepover and considered it a measure of success, like an asset to be listed on a personality résumé, to have been invited now. Never mind that it was a pity party for Michelle, an odd collection of freaks and misfits and loners Michelle's mother had cobbled together to encourage her daughter. The invitees were Selena, Helen, Chika, and a timid

Russian girl named Julia—the immigrants, possibly also the nerds; and the punks—Ruthie, Joan, and the tall, modelesque twins Laura and Alice, who despite perfect bone structure eschewed popularity with pink hair and spiked chokers from Hot Topic. Selena imagined proudly that her friendship with Ruthie was the bridge that brought these disparate groups together; in her brief middle school career, she had transformed from friendless new kid into a sort of cultural ambassador.

Selena's father had been skeptical—"What's the point of sleeping in someone else's house?"—but agreed with a shrug when Selena said Helen was going. He had met Helen's parents at the Chinese Baptist Church, where he sometimes took Selena on Sundays for the free lunch; Helen's mother was a mathematics professor at the university where he was getting his engineering degree. Helen was going, yes, but she and Chika were getting picked up at nine thirty and would not be staying overnight. Selena conveniently forgot to tell her father this.

It was the week before winter break. The ruse was a sort of holiday party. Michelle had invited them with a defeated smile.

"My mom . . . wants me to be like, normal . . ." She gave a weak laugh. "Anyways, I'm having a slumber party, it'll be fun!"

Since returning to school with bandaged wrists, Michelle had affected a meek cheerfulness, smiling with raised eyebrows and piping "Good mornings!" and "See yas!" in the halls. At lunch she sat behind the gym with her back against the bricks and cried silently, her tears not so much an expression of emotion as of inevitability, like water following gravity downhill. She peeled off her bandages and picked at the scabs of her scars. She still loved Samuel, but Samuel would not take her back, not now. Rumor was Samuel had called her a "fucking lunatic crazywoman" when he'd heard what she did and deleted her number.

"Please, he loves the attention," Ruthie had muttered.

It was Carol who had put her foot down. Carol, who did not really believe in disciplining children, did so now. She had forbidden her son from "torturing that poor girl further."

Carol talked about Michelle as she drove Ruthie and Selena to the slumber party, about poor Michelle and damned lost Samuel, who would take down G-d knew how many poor girls with him if she couldn't figure out how to get through to him. Selena had not been in Carol's van since closing night of the fall musical, after which the Rubins had gone to New York City for ten days over Thanksgiving to visit the extended family. New York City, where movies took place.

After New York, Ruthie had been distant and cool. She'd shrugged silently when Selena came to her with thoughts about *The Bell Jar*, which she had lent Selena while away. "Oh yeah, I didn't really like it either," Selena said, tossing the book back. "It was kinda dark?"

"You think *this* is dark?" Something had come into Ruthie's eyes. "You know, sometimes I can't stand how fucking fragile you are, Selena, like, I dunno, like I could shatter you with a freaking tap to the forehead." She laughed loudly and without humor. "Oh my god. Are you *crying*?"

Had Selena teared up? Had she stuttered, *I'm sorry*?

For a moment Ruthie had softened. "It's okay," she'd said, but she'd turned away. "You're just sheltered."

Selena imagined Ruthie in New York City, and the image in her mind's eye was Julia Roberts strolling down Park Avenue, the wind billowing out her red hair. In New York City, had Ruthie made the final slip into the grown-up world? Selena resolved not to be so easily left behind. The slumber party was an opportunity. Late into the night, she would lie down next to Ruthie. Their faces would turn toward each other in the dark. Ruthie would whisper about New York, and Selena would imbibe the glamour and lights into her own lungs like secondhand smoke.

"Be *kind* to her!" Carol reminded as they got out of the car. "Talk to her, be *nice*."

MICHELLE WAS NOT POOR, AS Selena had assumed. Michelle's mother greeted the girls with a tray of red and green pepper rods fanned around a delicate glass bowl of ranch dressing. She had blond hair and a syrupy, kind voice, and appeared to Selena like an image that had stepped out of the television. Selena craned her neck, gawking helplessly at the high ceiling of the entryway, the twinkling twelve-foot tree emerging from pyramids of gold-wrapped boxes, the snaking wooden staircase garlanded with lights that wound around a chandelier and led upstairs. Around the palace Michelle's mother led them, through the classroom-sized kitchen, across cream-tiled floors in whose shine Selena could see her own reflection, finally taking them through a door downstairs into the basement, which had been finished with a white carpet that gave plushly under Selena's shoes. Shoes! Horrified, Selena rushed to pull them off, her pity for Michelle transforming into bewilderment, before she saw that everyone else was wearing theirs, including Michelle's mother, who stood elegantly in brown heels. What was this magic carpet, so fine it dissolved any dirt tracked in from outside?

The girls sat scattered about a long leather sofa that curved around the edge of the enormous room; beneath Selena's bottom the cushion was soft and firm at once. A very large and flat TV played *The Real World* on mute. Michelle's mother set down the tray and took the girls' sleeping bags: Ruthie's purple nylon tube and a black garbage bag from Selena in which her father had stuffed her blanket and pillow.

They ate pizza and salad. Selena wondered if her father had delivered it. Selena wondered if her father had peered into the magnificent entryways of all her classmates' homes. Michelle's mother came down a few times to say something enthusiastically and take away the boxes and paper Santa plates. "So this is what happens at a sleepover," said Selena's mind at regular intervals.

"So this is what happens at a sleepover!" it said when Alice announced: "Time for Never Have I Ever!"

"Ooh, yes," Alice's twin cooed.

Sometime in the evening, the twins had taken over, emboldened by the general fear of their beauty. Michelle, most of all, seemed afraid of them.

"Seriously?" Ruthie rolled her eyes. "I'm out." She looked at Michelle: "You don't have to play if you don't want to."

"It's okay." Michelle gave a weak smile. "It'll be fun."

Ruthie left and for once Selena did not want to follow. She looked at Helen, who sat in a kind of thrall. She held out her ten fingers.

"Never have I ever sucked dick," said Alice.

"Guilty," said Laura, and put a finger down. "Never have I ever sucked Samuel Rubin's dick behind the gym."

They grinned at Michelle. If Selena had not been preoccupied with interpreting the meaning of these words, interpreting the rules of the game, preoccupied with the edge of exhilaration tightening her chest—*So this is what happens at a sleepover!*—she might have noticed that she had heard these phrases before, in the form of rumors about Michelle. Selena's ten fingers were all still up; she sensed this was nearly as shameful as putting a finger down at every round. And what would she say when her turn came? There was an art to this game, it was about not just exposing another's secrets but revealing your own worldliness while doing so.

"Uh, never have I ever flashed anyone?" said Chika.

"Never have I ever played Never Have I Ever," announced Helen. "Before now."

"Clever," Alice said, putting down a finger.

"Never have I ever . . ." Selena still had ten fingers up. "Never have I ever met my mother."

"Whoa, you're dark," Laura said. "I like it."

"Never have I ever had anal," Michelle offered. Nobody had had anal.

Quickly Michelle lost. Selena's vocabulary expanded with the inscrutable things Michelle had ever done: "sucked dick," "hand job in a car," "fingered at the movies," "gone all the way." She looked at Michelle with amazement. Was Michelle more daring, more advanced, even, than Ruthie? The more Selena looked at Michelle, the more she saw womanness emanate from her, not the oozing glittering womanness of Ruthie, but one that seemed old and calm and almost—wise? And where *was* Ruthie?

"Where the hell is Ruthie?" Laura said. Laura wanted to play Spin the Bottle, no bother that they didn't have boys. "I mean, Ruthie's bi, we can show we're cool with it," Laura said, and everyone agreed. "Cool with it" was the general theme of the night.

Selena was sent to fetch Ruthie. She stumbled through the maze of Michelle's house and found Ruthie on the floor of the walk-in closet between their sleeping bags. She plopped down beside her friend and pulled off Ruthie's headphones. "We're playing Spin the Bottle," she whispered in Ruthie's ear, to which Ruthie said, "Kissing more random people? No thanks." It was dark but she thought she saw Ruthie roll her eyes.

Coolly Ruthie began to speak of New York, of the boys she had met, of not just kissing but much more—everything Selena had wanted to know—but Selena could not focus, gripped by the feeling that she was in the wrong room, always, stuck in the room where nothing important was happening. Finally she understood that Ruthie had not just left her behind, but everyone. Forget Ruthie and all the people she'd kissed, Selena could not afford to miss her own opportunity; next time she played the Never game with or without Ruthie she would put a finger down for *something*. She returned to Spin the Bottle alone, just in time to see Chika close her eyes and pout her lips. Michelle put a hand around Chika's neck and pulled her in tenderly.

Kissing was not such a big deal, Selena learned. Kind of awkward actually, to press your lips against another dry set. Or perhaps it was because she had spun Joan, the least exciting one, even her name was dull. Too soon, Alice and Laura got bored. They disbanded, lounging about listlessly in search of topics of conversation. Selena clung close to Helen, who was talking quite naturally with Alice and Laura, talking and also staring, enthralled.

"Actually I've never been kissed before," Helen said without embarrassment. She looked at Laura. "You were my first kiss."

"No way," Alice said.

"That was not a real kiss," Laura said, laughing. "*This* is a real kiss."

Laura crawled over to Helen and cupped her face in her hands. Laura kissed Helen long and hard. Selena thought she saw Laura's tongue edge between Helen's teeth and the tip of it poking the insides of Helen's cheek. She might have said, *It was my first kiss too*, but if she did, she spoke too quietly for even herself to really hear. Finally Laura released stunned Helen. Selena had never seen her friend's face so red.

"Chiiiika, Heeellllllen!" Michelle's mother called from upstairs. "Your parents are here—say good night!"

THE SUMMER AFTER EIGHTH GRADE, Selena's father got his degree and a job at a computer parts company in a small town in the Northeast. Selena and her father packed their belongings into the back of the silver Toyota hatchback that still smelled like old pizza. Miraculously, everything fit. Helen Li came over to hug Selena goodbye and ran after the car waving. Selena watched out the back windshield until Helen was a hot blur, shrinking, and beside her, the dark knot of the unsaid and misheard that had only grown every time she'd tried to untangle it—they turned the corner and the last cord snapped. Selena felt dizzy, and strangely light.

For three days the road unfurled, broken only by stops at rest areas for leg stretching and reclined-seat naps, at Motel 6s and Super 8s for beds and continental breakfasts. From the passenger seat Selena unwrapped mealy bagels from cellophane and watched the unending yellow fields of corn and wheat fly by, then give way to clusters of skyscrapers that emerged beside the freeway and fell behind in a matter of blinks. On the last day the terrain tightened. The rare buildings grew more frequent, shrank and huddled together, and the freeway lanes multiplied; long-haul trucks pulled off to be replaced by hundreds of little cars.

In the new town, her father no longer delivered pizzas. Their two-bedroom apartment was driving distance to "the beach," a windy rockscape salted with cold Atlantic spray. At the new high school, which was smaller than her former middle school, Selena no longer qualified for free lunch, and nobody else did either. Selena was the only Chinese kid; besides one Black boy in the eleventh grade and an olive-skinned Greek girl, everyone was Pilgrim-white. Selena threw away her flooding Walmart jeans and got new flares from the juniors section of JCPenney. Finally, at the end of ninth grade, she got her period. "Take me to CVS now, it's an emergency," she announced to her father, and strode into the feminine hygiene aisle, triumphant. Soon after, she initiated herself into the world of padded A-cup bras.

She joined Choir and Drama, where she sometimes got small parts, and was encouraged to take private voice lessons by the music director. Her father agreed after some pleading, and soon Selena was competing as a classical vocalist, playing her voice like others played the violin, singing art songs before panels of judges and even, toward the end of high school, soaring on a Mozart aria about doomed love that took her to All-State. She was a coloratura soprano, her voice teacher said; in opera her voice was fit for the prima donna. Here was the role, finally, she had envisioned for herself: the canary in the cage, waiting for the radiant tenor to free her from the throes of the evil baritone. On cue he appeared, her first boyfriend, a nice white boy named Matthew, son of geography professors, with whom she would venture into the land of consensual firsts, Matthew treating her body with a gentle respect that made her furious with impatience. She tortured poor Matthew a little, breaking up with him out of sheer boredom only to declare her undying love months later when rumor said a certain Annie, slated to kiss Matthew onstage in the spring play, was nurturing a secret crush. Senior year she dreamed of auditioning for conservatory, but just when her father was on the verge of relenting, she got into Columbia, early decision; on the night before her flight to New York she greedily took Matthew's cherry and her own before bidding him good luck and forever farewell. She went and got educated. She learned how to dress, finally growing out of preteen awkwardness, growing into her small breasts and hipless figure, desirable now that she was no longer a girl. She learned how to properly kiss, to seduce, to be seduced, how to remember that she'd liked it, and to close into the dark zipped pouch between her vocal folds the sensation of shrinking skin. On her twenty-fifth birthday she was getting fingered against a glass wall in a hotel bar bathroom, the glittering city pressed flat into her face, by a graying man who whispered, pinching her tits, that most women were ruined by twenty-five, when, like that, she lost her will to promiscuity. By then she no longer sang; sometimes she filled journals with poems she showed no one. Was it a minor miracle that the following week, newly enrolled in hot yoga, newly committed to a diet cleanse—nothing but temple food—she rolled out her mat and towel next to who else but—Matthew? Dear Matthew! He lived down the street, was at NYU studying law; his baby fat had melted to reveal a strong jawline, now accentuated by a light chocolate stubble, while the slight lines and shadows that came from reading late into the night gave his face just enough gravitas—some days she looked at him in disbelief, like she'd gone dumpster diving and come out winning the lottery. In no time they were married and settled, in a two-bed, one-bath in the West Village, no less—he a corporate lawyer, she an assistant professor of English and the author of a book of poetry—sometimes Selena gazed out their French windows at the gray Hudson and wrote about how far she'd come.

With her old friends Selena had long lost touch. Toward the end of high school, Helen Li had called her out of the blue to ask where she'd been and demand she join Facebook, and from the lingering habit of obedience Selena had created an account. For some years she was aware of Helen on the corner of her computer screen as a vaguely known entity living life elsewhere. Helen never mentioned any of the old gang. Selena imagined they had disbanded after she left, Helen and Chika off to accelerated classes, Joan and Julia to mediocrity, Michelle and Alice and Laura and sometimes Ruthie spinning down dark, unsalvageable paths. She stayed on Facebook for long enough to watch Helen go to business school and get a job on Wall Street, the costume of which flattered her. Helen had chopped off her ponytail and now wore dolphin-gray Armani suits that presented her body like a little package of power. She'd married an Indian woman, a pediatrician with long silky hair. Pity, Selena thought idly, if they weren't gay their tiger parents might have been so proud. Then it became clear that Facebook was no force of good in Selena's life or in the life of the world; it weaseled into the pettiest parts of her and picked them out like artifacts of all she was. She deleted her account and gratefully renounced knowledge of the ghosts of her past lives.

ON THE FIFTH ANNIVERSARY OF their marriage, Matthew surprised Selena with tickets to the Metropolitan Opera, a throwback to their youth. Orchestra seats, a rare production of *Faust*. "Don't even tell me how much they cost," Selena said, elated nonetheless. She was pregnant, with a girl she felt, though they had agreed to keep it a surprise. She wore a black-and-silver Dior dress from the 1920s she had found in a consignment shop uptown, which soon would no longer fit, and a little feather and mesh-veiled hat. How good-looking we are, she thought as she ascended the red velvet staircase with her husband, circling the glittering orbs of the Swarovski chandelier. From the mezzanine of the Met the twinkling lights of cabs circling Lincoln Center could have belonged to Ford Model Ts or even to horse-drawn carriages. And if Selena extracted herself from the picture, well, the audience—or were they called patrons?—might have been from another time too. For a moment Selena felt in a mirage, transported to another skin. She shook herself. The knob of style had turned. Whereas in high school Selena had worn Matthew like a badge—*I too can have a white boyfriend*—now it was she who was worn proudly by Matthew, a corsage of culture and sophistication, granting him the ability to say at office parties and happy hours phrases like "Being in an interracial relationship myself . . ." She followed him into the magnificent theater, after the gracious usher, and took her seat.

The first notes of the overture sounded. Strings swelled and plunged. Mephistopheles blew into their ears, and in an instant, all were young. Selena remembered how music dislodged emotion and brought it to her brim. Happily she thought, I have always been a person who is moved by art! She shut her eyes as the strings sliced a chord and the first voice sang, and the spirits of nature and hell danced across the stage. How precious, that she had once wept before her father, begging him to let her audition for Juilliard, that she had said, "I've never wanted anything this much!" The future had been an open field then, opaque and blinding white; in the blindness a million paths waited to clarify into color and shape. She had not known enough to imagine what any one path might look like, or to understand that to take one might preclude your journey on another.

The soprano was singing. Her first treble cry—*Non, monsieur!*—floated into the theater, as if not from a single source but from the very air. The cymbals and brass that had been banging and hollering hushed, and so did Selena's thoughts. What a lovely voice. With her once-coloratura's ear, Selena admired the soprano, how she sang her highest notes with the lushness of a mezzo, giving them a bitter edge that made the sweet undertones almost impossible to bear. The voice was divine, ringing with effortless radiance, and the singer charismatic too: petite, yet her presence took up the entire stage. Here was talent, and skill, and a mysterious something Selena could not put her finger on—

Fumbling, she reached for her program. She thumbed through the pages for the insert announcing tonight's understudies, which had nearly fallen out as the lights dimmed; even before she brought the text close to her face in the low light and read the name, she knew.

Est-ce toi? the soprano sang at her reflection in a gold mirror. *Est-ce toi?*

Non, ce n'est plus toi!

Ruth Rubin was not as beautiful as in Selena's memory. She had dyed her hair blond, or perhaps was wearing a wig. Selena looked past the diamonds glittering around Ruth's pale neck and arms. The program had fallen to her feet. Were there wisps of red at the edges of the hairline, escaping from beneath, flaming in the light?

Selena leaned in, no longer watching the opera but watching for Ruthie—*her* Ruthie—to break through and replace this Ruth Rubin on the stage. She waited for the bath of recognition—*I knew her, really, I did!* Was it possible this was the first time she had watched her friend, really watched, without straining to see her own reflection? How astonishing this other person was, who had lived an entire other life, not as beautiful without the sheen of her envy, yet somehow more unbelievable. Selena saw now that Ruth employed her wildness, not the other way around, and this was what had always made her so thrilling to watch; if you pulled one pin out, she might unravel—you sat on the edge of your seat, waiting for the pin to fall, but it never did.

The cadenza sounded; the curtain fell slowly as Ruth gave a harried look to the audience from inside her seducer's embrace. The final chord of the act trailed off low and hesitant, drowning in the audience's roar. Selena sat back as the stage lights dimmed, still vaguely waiting. In the moment of pitch black, she glimpsed a faint image. The focus tuned; the image brightened. Then it was hurtling at her, solid and whole—when she realized it was not the memory she'd been searching for but another, a Ruthie stuffed away and mothballed in her dank drawers of self, it was too late:

They sat in a closet, backs against a dark wall, on the night of the slumber party.

"You really want to know about New York?"

Ruthie did not look at her but held her with another force, the force of Ruthie. Ruthie hugged her knees to her chest and stared straight ahead.

"Samuel and I were hanging out in the hotel," Ruthie was saying. "Some of his friends were over, in our room. They were drinking, they were on something. I was on stuff too. Samuel left to get more booze and drugs. His friends started messing around. They started joking about how easy it would be . . . how easy it would be to . . . I thought they were joking. It started as a joke. I laughed along. I laughed along but I was a little scared. They saw that I was scared. The more scared I got, the more excited they got. They got really excited."

Ruthie looked straight at her. Selena saw clearly now—her friend's eyes had been begging.

"Do you need me to say it?" Ruthie's voice echoed in the room.

Selena was a sieve. She tried to grasp the words but they fell through her. Now she heard someone say *rape*. Somebody kept saying *rape*. Selena inside Selena winced, as if she had been slapped. Her ears hummed. Faintly she understood she should be concerned, more: horrified, hollering—the terror of knowledge gripped her throat. At last she said: "What did you do?" She tried to inject her voice with what she felt, and it came out small and shrill. "Did you fight?"

The begging left Ruthie's eyes.

"I thought if I told you . . ." Ruthie blinked once and stood up. "Forget it."

She left the room.

THE LIGHTS CAME ON FOR INTERMISSION.

"Babe? Babe?"

Matthew was prodding her. The people sitting in the middle of their row stood waiting to get out, and Selena was the blockade that prevented them. Dazed, she held on to her husband's elbow and was lifted and led to the mezzanine.

"What do you think so far? It's superb, isn't it, the performance, and the production, I was just blown away by the set, those screens, and that moving floor," Matthew said. "Even the understudy who sings Marguerite is phenomenal, I mean, what stage presence, she walks on and even with all the costumes and lights your eyes can't help . . ."

"I knew her," Selena said weakly. "We went to middle school . . . She was my friend. She was. My best friend."

"Seriously? That's nuts!" Matthew grew more animated. "Who would have thought? And to think she was on tonight! You should have said! Should we go and say hi, I mean, should we try to get backstage or something?"

The frescoed walls were tilting. White-haired people in elegant clothes sipped from little plastic flutes of champagne. They were looking at Selena, staring, eyes pointed, walking toward her, coming dangerously close. What did they want from her? Selena gripped both of Matthew's hands. "I was a child," she whispered, to the black tips of his shoes. "I was a child," and the truth of the words damned her.

In the Event

In the event of an earthquake, I texted Tony, we'll meet at the corner of Chinaman's Vista, across from the cafe with the rainbow flag.

Jen had asked about our earthquake plan. We didn't have one. We were new to the city, if it could be called that. Tony described it to friends back home as a huge village. But very densely populated, I added, and not very agrarian. We had come here escaping separate failures on the opposite coast. Already the escape was working. In this huge urban village, under the dry bright sky, we were beginning to regard our former ambitions as varieties of regional disease, belonging to different climates, different times.

"Firstly," Jen said, "you need a predetermined meeting point. In case you're not together and cell service is clogged. Which it's likely to be. Because, you know, disasters."

Jen was the kind of person who said things like *firstly* and *because, disasters*. She was a local local, born and raised and stayed. Tony had met Jen a few years ago at an electronic music festival back east and introduced us, thinking we'd get along. She had been traveling for work. Somehow we stayed in touch. We shared interests: she worked as a tech consultant but composed music as a hobby; I made electronic folk songs with acoustic sounds.

"The ideal meeting place," Jen explained, "is outside, walkable from both your workplaces, and likely free of obstacles."

"Obstacles?"

"Collapsed buildings, downed power lines, blah blah hazmat, you know."

Chinaman's Vista was the first meeting place that came to mind. It was a big grassy field far from the water, on high ground. Cypress trees lined its edges. In their shade, you could sit and watch the well-behaved dogs of well-behaved owners let loose to run around. We had walked past it a number of times on our way from this place or that—the grocery store, the pharmacy, the taqueria—and commented on its charm with surprise, forgetting we'd come across it before. In the event of a significant earthquake, and the aftershocks that typically follow significant earthquakes, I imagined we would be safe there—from falling debris at least—as we searched through the faces of worried strangers for each other.

OTHER FORCES COULD SEPARATE OR kill us: landslides, tsunamis, nuclear war. I was aware that we lived on the side of a sparsely vegetated hill, that we were four miles from the ocean, a mile from the bay. To my alarmed texts Tony responded that if North Korea was going to bomb us, this region would be a good target: reachable by missile, home to the richest and fastest-growing industry in the world. Probably they would go for one of the cities south of us, he typed, where the headquarters of the big tech companies were based.

nuclear blast wind can travel at > 300 m/s, Tony wrote. Tony knew things like this.

He clarified: meters per second

which gives us

I watched Tony's avatar think.

approx 3 mins to find shelter after detonation

More likely we'd get some kind of warning x hours before the bomb struck. Jen had a car. She could pick us up, we'd drive north as fast as we could. Jen's aunt who lived an hour over the bridge had a legit basement, concrete reinforced during the Cold War.

I thought about the active volcano one state away, which, if it erupted, could cover the city in ash. One very large state away, Tony reminded me. But the ash that remained in the air might be so thick it obscured the sun, plunging this usually temperate coast into winter. I thought about the rising ocean, the expanding downtown at sea level, built on landfill. Tony worked in the expanding downtown. Was Tony a strong swimmer? I asked with two question marks. His response:

don't worry lil chenchen

if i die i'll die

I WAS LISTENING TO AN audiobook, on 1.75× speed, about a techno-dystopic future Earth under threat of annihilation from alien attack. The question was whether humans would kill each other first or survive long enough to be shredded in the fast-approaching weaponized supermassive black hole. Another question was whether humans would abandon life on Earth and attempt to continue civilization on spacecraft. Of course, there were not enough spacecraft for everyone.

When I started listening, it was at normal 1.0× speed. Each time I returned I switched the speed dial up by 0.25×. It was a gripping book, full of devices for sustaining mystery despite the obvious conclusion. I couldn't wait for the world to end.

TONY AND I WERE FUNDAMENTALLY different. What I mean is we sat in the world differently—he settling into the back cushions, noting with objective precision the grime or glamour of his surroundings, while I hovered, nervous, at the edge of my seat. Often, I felt—more often now—I couldn't even make it to the edge. Instead I flitted from one space to another, calculating whether I would fit, considering the cosmic feeling of unwelcome that emanated from wherever I chose to go.

On the surface Tony and I looked very much the same. We were more or less the same percentile in height and weight, and we both had thin, blank faces, their resting expressions betraying slight confusion and surprise. Our bodies were constructed narrowly of long brittle bones, and our skin, pale in previous gray winters, now tanned easily to the same dusty brown. We weren't only both Chinese; our families came from the same rural-industrial province south of Shanghai recently known for small-goods manufacturing. But in a long reversal of fortunes, his family, originally businesspeople who had fled to Hong Kong and then South Carolina, were now lower-middle-class second-generation immigrants, while my parents, born from starving peasant stock, had stayed in China through its boom and immigrated much later to the States as members of the highly educated elite.

Tony's family was huge. I guess mine was too, but I didn't know any of them. In this hemisphere I had my parents, and that was it.

A couple of years ago I did Thanksgiving with Tony's family. It was my first time visiting the house where he'd grown up. It was also the first time I had left my parents to celebrate a holiday alone. I tried not to guess what they were eating—Chinese takeout or leftover Chinese takeout. Even when I was around, my parents spent most of their time sitting in separate rooms, working.

"Chenchen!" his mother had cried as she embraced me. "We're *so* happy you could join us."

My arms rose belatedly, swiping the sides of her shoulders as she pulled away.

She said my name like an American. The rest of the family did too—in fact, every member of Tony's family spoke with varied degrees of southern drawl. It was very disorienting. In normal circumstances Tony's English was incredibly bland, neutered of history, like my own, but now I heard in it long-drawn diphthongs, wholesome curls of twang. Both his sisters had come. As had his three uncles and two aunts with their families, and two full sets of grandparents, his mom's mom recently remarried after his grandpa's death. I had never been in a room with so many Chinese people at once, but if I closed my eyes and just listened to the chatter, my brain populated the scene with white people wearing bandannas and jeans.

The turkey had been deep-fried in an enormous vat of oil. We had stuffing and cranberry sauce and ranch-flavored mashed potatoes (a Zhang family tradition), pecan and sweet potato and ginger pies. We drank beer cocktails (Bud Light and lemonade). No one regretted the lack of rice or soy sauce, or said with a disappointed sigh that we should have just ordered roast duck from Hunan Garden. It was loud. I shouted small talk and halfway introduced myself to various relatives as bursts of yelling and laughter erupted throughout the room. Jokes were told—jokes! I had never heard people who looked like my parents making so many jokes—plates clinked, drinks sloshed, moving chairs and shoes scuffed the floor with a pleasing busy beat.

In the middle of all this I was struck suddenly by a wave of mourning, though I wasn't sure for what. The sounds of a childhood I'd never had, the large family I'd never really know?

Perhaps it was the drink—I think the beer-ade was spiked with vodka—but I felt somehow that I was losing Tony then, that by letting myself know him in this way I had opened a door through which he might one day slip away.

In the corner of the room, the pitch of the conversation changed. Tony's teenage cousin Harriet was yelling at her mother while Tony's mom sat at her side shaking her head. Slowly the other voices in the room quieted until the tacit attention of every person was focused on this exchange. Others began to participate, some angry—"Don't you dare speak to your mother like this"—some conciliatory—"How about some pecan pie?"—some anxious—Harriet's little sister tugging on her skirt. Harriet pushed her chair back angrily from the table. A vase fell over, dumping flowers and gray water into the stuffing. Harriet stormed from the room.

For a moment it was quiet. In my pocket my phone buzzed. By the time I took it out, the air had turned loud and festive again. this happens every year, Tony had texted. I looked at him; he shrugged with resigned amusement. Around me I heard casual remarks of a similar nature: comments on Harriet's personality and love life—apparently she had just broken up with a boyfriend—and nostalgic reminiscences of the year Tofu the dog had peed under the table in fright. It was like a switch had been flipped. In an instant the tension was diffused, injury and grievance transformed into commotion and fond collective memory.

I saw then how Tony's upbringing had prepared him for reality in a way that mine had not. His big family was a tiny world. It reflected the real world with uncanny accuracy—its little charms and injustices, its pettinesses and usefulnesses—and so, real-worldly forces struck him with less intensity, without the paralyzing urgency of assault. He did not need to survive living like I did, he could simply live.

I WOKE UP TO TONY'S phone in my face.

r u OK? his mom had texted. Followed by:

R U OK????

pls respond my dear son

call ASAP love mom (followed by heart emojis and, inexplicably, an ice cream cone)

His father and siblings and aunts and cousins and childhood friends had flooded his phone with similar messages. He scrolled through the unending ribbon of notifications sprinkled with news alerts. I turned on my phone. It gave a weak buzz. Jen had texted us at 4:08 A.M.:

did you guys feel the earthquake? i ran outside and left the door open and now i cant find prick

*pickle

Pickle was Jen's cat.

A lamp had fallen over in the living room. We had gotten it at a garage sale and put it on a stool to simulate a tall floor lamp. Now it was splayed across the floor, shade bent, glass bulb dangling but miraculously still intact. When we lifted it we saw a dent in the floorboards. The crooked metal frame of the lamp could no longer support itself and so we laid it on its side like a reclining nude. There were other reclining forms too. Tony had put toy action figures among my plants and books; all but Wolverine had fallen on their faces or backs. He sent a photo of a downed Obi-Wan Kenobi to his best nerd friends back home.

He seemed strangely elated. That he would be able to say, *Look, this happened to us too*, and without any real cost.

Later, while Tony was at work, I pored over earthquake preparedness maps on the internet. Tony's office was in a converted warehouse with large windows on the edge of the expanding downtown. On the map, this area was marked in red, which meant it was a liquefaction zone. I didn't know what liquefaction meant but it didn't sound good. Around lunchtime Tony sent me a YouTube video showing a tray of vibrating sand, on which a rubber ball bobbed in and out as if through waves in a sea. He'd forgotten about the earthquake already; his caption said, SO COOL. I messaged back: when the big one hits, you're the rubber ball.

That afternoon, I couldn't stop seeing his human body, tossed in and out through the rubble of skyscrapers. I reminded myself that Tony had a stable psyche. He was the kind of person you could trust not to lose his mind, not in a disruptive way, at least. But I didn't know if he had a strong enough instinct for self-preservation. Clearly, he didn't have a good memory for danger. And he wasn't resourceful, at least not with physical things like food and shelter. His imagination was better for fantasy than for worst-case scenarios.

I messaged:

if you feel shaking, move away from the windows. get under a sturdy desk and hold on to a leg. if there is no desk or table nearby crouch by an interior wall. whatever you do, cover your neck and head AT ALL TIMES

He sent me a sideways heart. I watched his avatar think and type for many moments.

I'm SERIOUS, I wrote.

Finally he wrote back:

umm what if my desk is by the window

. . .

should I get under the desk or go to an interior wall

I typed: get under your desk and push it to an interior wall while covering your head and neck. I imagined the rubber ball. I imagined the floor undulating, dissolving into sand. I typed: hold on to any solid thing you can.

I COULDN'T FOCUS ON WORK. I had recorded myself singing a series of slow glissandos in E minor, which I was trying to distort over a cello droning C. It was supposed to be the spooky intro before the drop of an irregular beat. The song was about failure's various forms, the wild floating quality of it. I wanted to show Tony I understood what he had gone through back east, at least in its primal movement and shape, that despite the insane specificity of his suffering he was not alone.

Now all I could hear were the vibrations of sand, the movements of people and buildings falling.

I went to the hardware store. I bought earthquake-proof cabinet latches and brackets to bolt our furniture to the walls. According to a YouTube video called "Seeing with Earthquake Eyes," it was best to keep the bed at least fifteen feet from a window or glass or mirror—anything that could shatter into sharp shards over your soft sleeping neck. Our bed was directly beneath the largest window in the apartment, which looked out into a dark shaft between buildings. The room was small; I drew many diagrams but could not find a way to rearrange the furniture. Fifteen feet from the window would put our bed in the unit next door. I bought no-shatter seals to tape over the windows. I assembled the necessary things for an emergency earthquake kit: bottled water, instant ramen, gummy vitamins. Flashlight, batteries, wrench, and a cheap backpack to hold everything. I copied our most important contacts from my phone and laminated two wallet-sized emergency contact cards in case cell service or electricity went down.

I bought a whistle for Tony. It blew at high C, a pitch of urgency and alarm. I knew he would never wear it. I'd make him tie the whistle to the leg of his desk. If the sand and ball video was accurate, and a big earthquake struck during business hours, there was a chance Tony would end up buried in a pile of rubble.

I imagined him alive, curled under the frame of his desk. In this scenario, the desk would have absorbed most of the impact and created a small space for him to breathe and crouch. He would be thirsty, hungry, afraid. I imagined his dry lips around the whistle, and the dispirited emergency crews layers of rubble above him, leaping up, shouting, "Someone's down there! Someone's down there!"

SUDDENLY I REMEMBERED I HAD forgotten to text Jen back.

> did u look in the dryer? or that box in the garage?
> everything ok over here thanks just one broken lamp

It'd taken me five hours to text Jen, yet now I was worried about her lack of instant response.

> did u find pickel? let me know i can come over and helpyou look
> maybe she's stuck in a tree??
> tony can print out some flyers at his office let me know!!!

I was halfway through enlarging a photo of Pickle I'd dug up from Google Photos when my phone buzzed.

> found pickle this morning in bed almost sat on her
> she was under the covers barely made a bump

She sent me a photo. Pickle was sitting on a pillow, fur fluffed, looking like a super grouch.

MY OFFICE HAD NO WINDOWS. It was partially underground, the garage-adjacent storage room that came with our apartment. We had discarded everything when we moved, so we had nothing to store. The room had one electrical outlet and was just big enough for my recording equipment and a piano. It was soundproof and the internet signal was weak. The recordings I made in there had a muffled, amplified quality, like a loud fight heard through a door.

The building where Tony and I rented was old, built in the late nineteenth century, a dozen years before the big earthquake. It had survived that one, but still by modern building codes it was what city regulators called a soft-story property. According to records at city hall, it had been seismically retrofitted by mandate five years ago. I saw evidence of these precautions in the garage: extra beams and girding along the foundations, the boilers and water tanks bolted to the walls. I couldn't find my storage/work room on any of the blueprints. Tony thought I was hypocritical to keep working there, given my new preoccupation with safety. I liked the idea of making music in a place that didn't technically exist, even if it wasn't up to code.

Or maybe it was. I imagined, in fact, that the storage rooms had been secret bunkers—why else was there a power outlet? I felt at once safe and sober inside it, this womb of concrete, accompanied by the energies of another age of panic. Now I filled the remaining space with ten gallons of water (enough for two people for five days); boxes of Shin noodles and canned vegetable soup; saltine crackers; tins of Spam; canned tuna for Tony, who no longer ate land animals; a small camping stove I found on sale. I moved our sleeping bags and our winter coats down.

My office, my bunker. More and more it seemed like a good place to sit out a disaster. If we ran out of bottled water, the most vital resource, there stood the bolted water heaters, just a few steps away.

"HOLY SHIT," TONY SAID WHEN he came home from work. "Have you seen the news?"

I pursed my lips. I didn't read the news anymore. The sight of the new president's face made me physically ill. Instead I buried myself in old librettos and scores, spent whole days listening to the kind of music that made every feeling cell in my brain vibrate with forgetting: Bach, Bach, and more Bach. I'd listen to Glenn Gould huffing and purring through the Goldberg Variations and think, All the human mind needs is one perfect theme, to wind and wind and wind around itself to keep it from unraveling.

Tony did the opposite. Once upon a time he had been a consumer of all those nonfiction tomes about social and historical issues vying for the Pulitzer Prize. He used to send me articles that took multiple hours to read—I'd wondered when he ever did work. Now he only sent me tweets.

He waved his phone in my face.

Taking up the entire screen was a photograph of what appeared to be hell. Hell, as it appeared in medieval paintings and Hollywood films. Hills and trees burning so red they appeared liquid, the sky pulsing with black smoke. A highway cut through the center of this scene, and on the highway, impossibly, were cars, fleeing and entering the inferno at top speed.

"This is Loma," Tony said.

"Loma?"

"It's an hour from here? We were there last month?"

"We were?"

"That brewery with the chocolate? Jen drove?"

"Oh. Yeah. Wow."

According to the photograph's caption, the whole state was on fire. Tony's voice was incredulous, alarmed.

"Have you gone outside today?"

I hadn't.

We walked to Chinaman's Vista, where there was a view of the city. Tony held my hand and I was grateful for it. The air was smoky, it smelled like everyone was having a barbecue. If I closed my eyes I could imagine I was in my grandmother's village in

Zhejiang, those hours before dinner when families started firing up their wood-burning stoves.

"People are wearing those masks," Tony said. "Look—like we're in fucking Beijing."

Tony had never been to Beijing. I had. The smog wasn't half as bad as this.

We sat on a bench in Chinaman's Vista and looked at the sky. The sun was setting. Behind the gauze of smoke it was a brilliant salmon orange, its light so diffused you could stare straight at it without hurting your eyes. The sky was pink and purple, textured with plumes of color. It was the most beautiful sunset I had ever seen. Around us the light cast upon the trees and grass and purple bougainvillea an otherworldly yellow glow, more nostalgic than any Instagram filter. I looked at Tony, whose face had relaxed in the strange beauty of the scene, and it was like stumbling upon a memory of him—his warm, dry hand clasping mine, the two of us looking and seeing the same thing.

TONY'S FAILURE HAD TO DO with the new president. He had been working on the opposing candidate's campaign, building what was to be a revolutionary technology for civic engagement. They weren't only supposed to win. *They* were the ones who were supposed to go down in history for changing the way politics used the internet.

My failure had to do with Tony. I had failed to save him, after.

Tony had quit his lucrative job to work seven days a week for fifteen months at a quarter of the pay. The week leading up to the election, he had slept ten hours total, five of them at headquarters, facedown on his desk. He didn't sleep for a month after, though not for lack of time. If there was ever a time for Tony to go insane, that would have been it.

Instead he shut down. His engines cooled, his fans stopped whirring, his lights blinked off. He completed the motions of living but his gestures were vacant, his eyes hollow. It was like all the emotions insisting and contradicting inside him had short-circuited some processing mechanism. In happier times, Tony had joked about his desire to become an android. "Aren't we already androids?" I asked, indicating the eponymous smart-phone attached to his hand. Tony shook his head in exasperation. "Cyborgs," he said. "You're thinking of cyborgs." He explained that cyborgs were living organisms with robotic enhancements. Whereas androids were robots made to be indistinguishable from the alive. Tony had always believed computers superior to humans—they didn't need to feel.

In this time I learned many things about Tony and myself, two people I had thought I already knew very well. At our weakest, I realized, humans have no recourse against our basest desires. For some this might have meant gorging in sex and drink, or worse—inflicting violence upon others or themselves. For Tony it meant becoming a machine.

BECAUSE OF THE WILDFIRE SMOKE, we were warned to go out-side as little as possible. This turned out to be a boon for my productivity. I shut myself in my bunker and worked.

I woke to orange-hued cityscapes. In the mornings I drank tea and listened to my audiobook. Earth was being shredded, infinitely, as it entered the supermassive black hole, while what remained of humanity sped away on a light-speed ship. "It's strangely beautiful," one character said as she looked back at the scene from space. "No, it's terrible," another said. The first replied: "Maybe beauty is terrible." I thought the author didn't really understand beauty or humans, but he did understand terror and time, and maybe that was enough. I imagined how music might sound on other planets, where the sky wasn't blue and grass wasn't green and water didn't reflect when it was clear. I descended to my bunker and worked for the rest of the day. I stopped going upstairs for lunch, not wanting to interrupt my flow. I ate dry packets of ramen, crumbling the noodle squares and munching on the pieces like potato chips. When I forgot to bring down a thermos of tea I drank the bottled water.

Fires were closing in on the city from all directions; fire would eat these provisions up. The city was surrounded on three sides by water—that still left one entry by land. It was dry and getting hotter by the day. I thought the city should keep a ship with emergency provisions anchored in the bay. I thought that if a real disaster struck, I could find it in myself to loot the grocery store a few blocks away.

In the evenings, Tony took me upstairs and asked about my workday. In the past he had wanted to hear bits of what I was working on; now he nodded and said, "That sounds nice." I didn't mind. I didn't want to share this new project with him— with anyone—until it was done. We sat on the couch and he showed me pictures of the devastation laying waste to the land. I saw sooty silhouettes of firefighters and drones panning gridwork streets of ash. I saw a woman in a charred doorway, an apparition of color in the black and gray remains of her home.

Once Jen came over to make margaritas. She put on one of Tony's Spotify playlists. "I'm sorry," she said, "I really need to unwind." She knew I didn't like listening to music while other noises were happening. My brain processed the various sounds into separate channels, pulling my consciousness into multiple tracks and dividing my present self. For Jen, overstimulation was a path to relaxation. She crushed ice and talked about the hurricanes ravaging the other coast, the floods and landslides in Asia and South America, the islands in the Pacific already swallowed by the rising sea.

Jen's speech, though impassioned, had an automatic quality to it, an unloading with a mechanical beat. I sipped my margarita and tried to converge her rant with the deep house throbbing from the Sonos: it sounded like a robot throwing up. Tony came home from work and took my margarita. Together they moved from climate change to the other human horrors I'd neglected from the news—ethnic cleansings, mass shootings, trucks mowing down pedestrians. They listed the newest obscenities of the new president, their voices growing louder and faster as they volleyed headlines and tweets. In the far corner of the couch, I hugged my knees. More and more it seemed to me that the world Jen and Tony lived in was one hysterical work of poorly written fiction—a bad doomsday novel—and that what was really real was the world of my music. More and more I could only trust those daytime hours when my presence coincided completely with every sound I made and heard.

I WAS MAKING A NEW album. I was making it for me but also for Tony, to show him it was still possible, in these times, to maintain a sense of self.

My last album had come out a year ago. I had been on tour in Europe promoting it when the election came and went. At the time I had justified the scheduling: Tony would want to celebrate with his team anyway, I would just get in the way. Perhaps I had been grateful for an excuse. On the campaign, Tony had been lit with a blind passion I'd never been able to summon for tangible things. I'd understood it—how else could you will yourself to work that much?—I'd even lauded it, I'd wanted his candidate to win too. Still, the pettiest part of me couldn't help resenting his work like a mistress resents a wife. I imagined the election night victory party as the climax of a fever dream, after which Tony would step out, cleansed, and be returned to me.

Of course, nothing turned out how I'd imagined.

My own show had to go on.

I remember calling Tony over Google Voice from backstage between shows, at coffee shops, in the bathroom of the hotel room I shared with Amy the percussionist—wherever I had Wi-Fi. I remember doing mental math whenever I looked at a clock—what time was it in America, was Tony awake? The answer, I learned, was yes. Tony was always awake. Often he was drunk. He picked up the phone but did not have much to say. I pressed my ear against the screen and listened to him breathe.

I remember Amy turning her phone to me: "Isn't this your boyfriend?" We were on a train from Brussels to Amsterdam. I saw Tony's weeping face, beside another weeping face I knew: Jen's. I zoomed out. Jen's arms were wrapped around Tony's waist; Tony's arm hugged her shoulders. The photograph was in a listicle published by a major American daily showing the losing candidate's supporters on election night, watching the results come in. I remembered that Jen had flown in to join Tony at the victory arena: in order to be "a witness to history." The photo list showed the diversity of the supporters: women in headscarves, disabled people, gay couples. Tony and Jen killed two birds with one stone: Asian America, and an ostensibly mixed-race couple. Jen was half-Chinese but she looked exotic-white—Italian, or Greek.

That night I'd called Tony. "How are you?" I'd asked as usual, and then: "I was thinking maybe I should just come back. Should I come back? I hate this tour." There was a long silence. Finally Tony said, "Why?" In his voice a mutter of cosmic emptiness.

I have one memory of sobbing under bright white lights, some terrible noise cracking into speakers turned too high. This might have been a dream.

For a long time after, I was estranged from music. What feelings normally mediated themselves in soundscapes, a well I could plumb for composition, hit me with their full blunt force.

Now I was trying to reenter music by making it in a new way, the way I imagined a sculptor makes a sculpture, to work with sound as if it were a physical material. Music was undoubtedly my medium: I had perfect pitch, a nice singing voice, and I liked the monasticism and repetition of practice. According to my grandmother, I had sung the melodies of nursery songs a whole year before I learned to speak. But I had the temperament of a conceptual artist, not a musician. Specifically, I was not a performer. I hated every aspect of performing: the lights, the stage, the singular attention. Most of all I could not square with the irreproducibility of performance—you had one chance, and then the work disappeared—which, to be successful, required a kind of faith. The greatest performers practiced and practiced, controlling themselves with utmost discipline, and when they stepped onto the stage, gave themselves over to time.

I wanted to resolve this contradiction by making music in a way that folded performance theoretically into composition. Every sound and silence in this album would be a performance. I would compose a work and perform it for myself, just once. From this material I would build my songs. If the recording didn't turn out, I abandoned the mistakes or used them. I didn't think about whom the music was for. Certainly not for a group of people to enjoy with dance, as my previous album had been—I too had been preparing for celebration. My new listener sat in an ambient room, alone, and simply let the sounds come in.

IN THE MORNING, TONY SHOWED me a video of three husky puppies doing something adorable. "Look," he said, pointing up and out the window. From the light well we could see a sliver of blue.

We got up and confirmed that the smoke had lifted. Tony reported from Twitter that the nearest fire had indeed been tamed. "Huzzah!" I said. I walked outside to wait with him for his UberPool to work. The sun was shining, the air was fresh, the colors of this relentlessly cheerful coast restored. I kissed him on the cheek goodbye.

I watched his car drive away and couldn't bear the thought of going back inside. My legs itched. I wanted—theoretically—to run. I put in earbuds and turned on my audiobook. I walked around the neighborhood, looking happily at the bright houses and healthy people and energetically pooping dogs.

In the audiobook, things had also taken a happy turn. The lady protagonist, who had escaped Earth on a light-speed ship, found herself reunited in a distant galaxy with the man who'd proved his unfailing love by secretly gifting her an actual star. This reunion despite the fact that eight hundred years had passed (hibernation now allowed humans to jump centuries of time) and that when they had last seen each other, the man's brain was being extracted from his body in order to be launched into outer space (it was later intercepted by aliens who reconstructed his body from the genetic material). She had discovered his love in that final moment, when it was too late to stop the surgery— besides then, the two had barely spoken—now he was finally to be rewarded for his devotion and patience. I thought the author had an exciting imagination when it came to technology but a shitty imagination for love. I found the endurance of this love story more unbelievable than the leaps in space and time.

That afternoon I tried to work but didn't get very much done. dinner out? I texted Tony. For the first time in a long time I wanted to feel like I lived in a city. I wanted to shower and put on mascara and pants that had a zipper.

Tony had a work event. I texted Jen. sry have a date! she wrote back, followed by a winking emoji that somehow seemed to say: *Ooh-la-la.*

I decided to go out to dinner alone. I listened to my audiobook over a plate of fancy pizza, shoveling down the hot dough as I turned up the speed on my book. By the time I finished the panna cotta, the universe was imploding, every living and non-living thing barreling toward the end of its existence. I looked at my empty plate as the closing credits came on to a string cadenza in D minor. I took out my earbuds and looked around the restaurant, at the redwood bar where I was sitting, the waitstaff in black aprons, the patrons in wool sneakers and thin down vests, the Sputnik lamps hanging above us all. Would I miss any of this? Yes, I thought, and then, just as fervently—I don't know.

Outside, the sky was fading to pale navy, a tint of yellow on the horizon where the sun had set. A cloudless, unspectacular dusk. I walked to dissipate the unknowing feeling and found myself at Chinaman's Vista, which was louder than I had ever heard it, everyone taking advantage of the newly particulate-free outdoors. I weaved through the clumps of people, looking at and through them, separate and invisible, like a visitor at a museum. That was when I saw, under a cypress tree, a woman who looked exactly like Jen, wearing Jen's gold loafers and pink bomber jacket. Jen was with a man. Jen was kissing the man. The man looked exactly like Tony.

I was breathing quickly. Staring. I wanted to run away but my feet were as glued as my eyes. Tony kissed Jen differently from how he kissed me. He grabbed her lower back with two hands and lifted her up slightly, while curling his neck to her upwardly lifted face. Because Jen was shorter than him. This made sense. I, on the other hand, was just about Tony's height.

I blinked and shook my head. Jen wasn't shorter than Tony. She was taller than us both. Jen and Tony stopped kissing and started to walk toward me, and I saw that it wasn't Tony, it was some other Asian guy who only kind of looked like Tony, but really not at all. Horrified, I turned and walked with intentionality to a plaque ahead on the path. I stared intently at the words and thought how the guy wasn't Tony and the girl probably wasn't even Jen, how messed up that I saw a white-ish girl with an East Asian guy and immediately thought Jen and Tony.

"Chenchen!"

It *was* Jen. I looked up with relief and dread. Jen stood on the other side of the plaque with her date, waving energetically.

"This is Kevin," she said. She turned to Kevin. "Chenchen's the friend I was telling you about, the composer-musician-*artiste*. She just moved to the city."

"Hey," I said. I looked at the plaque. "Did you know," I said, "Chinaman's Vista used to be a mining camp? For, uh, Chinese miners. They lived in these barrack-like houses. Then they were killed in some riots and maybe buried here, because, you know, this place has good feng shui." I paused. I'd made up the part about feng shui. The words on the plaque said *mass graves*. "This was back in the—1800s."

"Oh, like the gold rush?" Kevin said. His voice was deep, hovering around a low F. Tony spoke in the vicinity of B-flat. I looked up at him. He was much taller than Tony.

"Yeah," I said.

I stood there for a long time after they left, reading and rereading the historical landmark plaque, wishing I could forget what it said. Chinaman's Vista, I thought, was a misleading name.

The view was of cascading expensive houses, pruned and prim. The historic Chinese population, preferring squalor and cheap rents, had long since relocated to the other side of town. Besides me and possibly Kevin and half of Jen, there weren't many living Chinese people here.

WHAT WAS WRONG WITH ME? Why didn't I want to be a witness to history, to any kind of time passing?

THE TEMPERATURE SKYROCKETED. TONY AND I kicked off our blankets in sleep. We opened the windows and the air outside was hot too. Heat radiated from the highway below in waves. The cars trailed plumes of scorching dust.

Tony texted me halfway through the day to say it was literally the hottest it had ever been. I clicked the link he sent and saw a heat map of the city. It was 105 degrees in our neighborhood, 101 at Tony's work. We didn't have an air conditioner. We didn't, after all my disaster prep, even have a fan. Tony's work didn't have A/C either. Nobody in the city did, I realized when I left the house, searching for a cool cafe. Every business had its doors wide open. Puny ceiling fans spun as fast as they could but only pushed around hot air. It was usually so fucking temperate here, the weather so predictably perfect. I walked past melting incredulous faces: women in leather boots, tech bros carrying Patagonia fleeces with dismay.

My phone buzzed. Jen had sent a photo of what looked like an empty grocery store shelf. It buzzed again.

the fan aisle at Target!!

just saw a lady attacking another lady for the last $200 tower fan

#endofdays?

That weekend, I took Tony to the mall. Tony had been sleeping poorly, exasperated by my body heat. He was sweaty and irritable and I felt somehow responsible. I felt, I think, guilty. Since the incident at Chinaman's Vista I'd been extra nice to Tony.

The A/C in the mall wasn't cold enough. A lot of people had had the same idea. "Still better than being outside," I said hopefully as we stepped onto the crowded escalator. Tony grunted his assent. We walked around Bloomingdale's. I pointed at the mannequins wearing wool peacoats and knitted vests and laughed. Summer in the city was supposed to be cold, because of the ocean fog. Tony said, "Ha ha."

We got ice cream. We got iced tea. We got texts from PG&E saying that power was out on our block due to the grid overheating, would be fixed by 8 P.M. We weren't planning to be back until after sunset anyway, I said. I looked over Tony's shoulder at his phone. He was scrolling through Instagram, wistfully it seemed, through photographs of Jen and other girls in bikinis—they had gone to the beach. "But you don't like the beach," I said. Tony shrugged. "I don't like the mall either," he said. I asked if he wanted to go to the beach. He said no.

We ate salads for dinner and charged our phones. This, at last, seemed to make Tony happy. "In case the power is still out later," he said. We sat in the food court and charged our phones until the mall closed.

THE APARTMENT WAS A CACOPHONY of red blinking eyes. The appliances had all restarted when the power came back on. Now they beeped and hummed and buzzed, imploring us to reset their times. Outside the wide-open windows, cars honked and revved their engines. So many sounds not meant to be simultaneous pressed simultaneously onto me. In an instant the cheerfulness I'd mustered for our wretched day deflated. I found myself breathing fast and loud, tears welling against my will. Tony sat me down and put his noise-canceling headphones over my ears. "I can still hear everything!" I shouted. I could hear, I wanted to say, the staticky G-sharp hiss of the headset's noise-canceling mechanism. Tony was suddenly contrite. He handed me a glass of ice water and shushed me tenderly. He walked around the apartment, re-setting all our machines.

We took a cold shower. Tony looked as exhausted as I felt. We kept the lights off and went directly to bed. Traffic on the highway had slowed to a rhythmic whoosh. I wanted to hug Tony but it was too hot. I took his hand and released it. Our palms were sweaty and gross.

I was just falling asleep when I heard a faint beep.

I nudged Tony. "What was that?" He rolled away from me. I turned over and closed my eyes.

It beeped again, then after some moments, again.

It was a high C, a note of shrill finality. I counted the beats between: about 20 at 60 bpm. I counted to twenty, hoping to lull myself to sleep. But the anticipation of the coming beep was too much. My heart rate rose, I counted faster, unable to maintain a consistent rhythm, so now it was 22 beats, then 25, then 27.

Finally I sat up, said loudly: "Tony, Tony, do you hear the beeping?"

"Huh?" He rubbed his eyes. It beeped again, louder, as if to back me up. Tony got up and poked at the alarm clock, which he hadn't reset because it ran on batteries. He pulled the batteries out and threw them to the floor. He lay down, I thanked him, and then—*beep*.

I sat on the bed, clamping my pillow over my ears, and watched Tony lumber about the dark bedroom, drunk with exhaustion, finding every hidden gadget and extracting its batteries, taking down even the smoke detector. Each time it seemed he had finally identified the source, there sounded another beep. It was a short sound, it insisted then disappeared; even my impeccable hearing could not locate from where exactly it came. It sounded as if from all around us, from the air. Tony fell on the bed, defeated. He said, "Can we just try to sleep?" We clamped our eyes shut, forced ourselves to breathe deeply, but the air was agitated and awake. My mind drifted and ebbed, imitating the movements of sleep while bringing nothing like rest. I couldn't help thinking that the source of the sound was neither human nor human-made. I couldn't help imagining the aliens in my audiobook preparing to annihilate our world. "Doomsday clock," I said, half-aloud. I was thinking or dreaming of setting up my equipment to record the beeps. I was thinking or dreaming of unrolling the sleeping bags in my bunker, where it'd be silent and I could sleep. "Counting down."

"I'm sorry," Tony said.

"It's okay," I said, but it wasn't, not really, and Tony knew it. He grabbed my hand and squeezed it hard. Between the cosmic beeps his lips smacked open as if to speak, as if searching for the right words to fix me. Finally he said, "I kissed Jen," and I said, "I know."

Then: "What?"

Then: "When?"

My eyes were wide open.

"Last November."

High C sounded, followed by ten silent beats.

"You were in Germany."

Another high C. Twenty beats. Another high C.

"I'm sorry," Tony said again. "Say something, please?" He tightened his hand. I tried to squeeze back to say I'd heard, I was awake. I failed. I listened to the pulses of silence, the inevitable mechanical beeps.

"Tell me what you're thinking?"

I was thinking we would need a new disaster meetup spot. I was wondering if there was any place in this city, this world, where we'd be safe.

The Garden

On the other side of the world a small hole had opened in her grandmother's mind and memories were dripping out one by one. Meanwhile the airports were shut and they were told to also shut their doors. They were told not to concern themselves with any but the ones inside these shut doors; it was the law. Herself, and a little dog. Two souls were plenty, enough to sometimes feel like too much. News came by images on screens, as did diversion and entertainment, the pulse of the greater world. The woman had spilled coffee and fizzled one screen to black. She laughed. What had seemed to contain her life in entirety was now an obvious scrap of metal. On a smaller screen, in the palm of her hand, she watched her grandmother eating loquats.

Intently her grandmother ate, biting into the fruit and spitting the seeds and skin onto the floor. Every so often a hand reached into the image to wipe the residue from her chin. "We grew these, in the garden," said the owner of the hand—her cousin Lulu. As their grandmother ate, Lulu spoke of her condition and of the condition of the garden, of the saplings that now bore fruit. Every so often their grandmother looked up into the camera and said with relish, "The loquats are very sweet."

How the woman wished to eat a loquat too. To bite into the firm flesh, to meet the smooth pit with her teeth. On her tongue, a taste stitched so deep in the sense-world of her childhood it was not accompanied by a memory of eating. When had she acquired this taste? Or was she born with it? What she remembered was learning to paint loquats, the summer after Lulu was born. Her grandmother walked her to the lessons, which took place in the back of a paint shop on Arts and Letters Lane. Her grandmother held her hand and carried sleeping Lulu in her free arm, Lulu who cried madly that summer unless cocooned in the comfort of another's embrace.

Loquats were the second lesson, after you'd mastered the stalks and leaves of bamboo. You held the brush upright and kissed it to the paper, then gave a small twirl of the wrist. The teacher was exacting; the girl blotted many tissue-thin pages with gray-black swirls before he cut open the tube of yellow ink. Then the loquats sat there on the paper looking so plump and so sweet. She twirled her wrist and the craving entered her mouth.

So that was childhood. In the insular rhythms of these shut-door days she returned to the cadence of another childhood, after the ocean had been crossed, the cadence of being alone. Receiving news of the greater world and her smaller one by messages detached from bodies. Now there was the capability of technology, conveying the image of your grandmother's body; in childhood the images had existed only in memory. Her first knowledge of death had been in this way imaginary: words and tears over the telephone; years later, a long journey to a grave. The real existing in the gap between. So what? She knew how to be happy here, enclosed in the four walls of her mind.

One day, she discovered a loquat tree in her neighborhood. With amazement she went to it, exclaiming "Can you believe it" again and again to the dog. The tree stood inside the enclosed courtyard of a large blue house on the hip of a hill mere blocks from where she lived. Its branches reached over the iron spokes of the fence, shading the sidewalk, and they were heavy with fruit. There loquats hung, yellow and orange, clinging to the fists of the branches. She reached to pluck one but it was too high; the branch pulled away laughing as her hand went up. The dog sniffed at the air, twitching its wet black nose. She tugged off her mask and put her nose up too. Into her nostrils barreled the exhaust of a truck gunning by, windows down, the driver shouting incomprehensibly over its roar—"Go back to your country"? A spit wad landed impressively near her feet.

Daily she sought the tree. She could never remember exactly where it was. With the dog at her side she circled the blocks until she spotted the dark blue roof, the iron spokes puncturing the pale sky. She looked at the dog and said, "Let's go." Noses up, they went. Still the fruit was beyond their reach. She had taught the dog to jump on her command. Together they jumped; together the branches snatched back their hands. She landed, dejected. The dog looked at her happily. How she wished to be like the dog, pure with joy and instinct. Her sweetness unpunctured by regret over what could not be achieved.

On the topmost branches the loquats had turned deep orange, on the brink of shrivel and rot. She looked into the yard for evidence of tending: a basket, a ladder, some kind of tool that lengthened the arm. She would be cheered to know that a gardener lived here. She would be satisfied knowing that even if she could not taste this fruit, somebody might. From the lowest branch hung—no, it was a swing. Who lived in this house, who watched this abundance ripen and die? Did they know these fruits were sweet?

Like this, the days. The bliss of a tiny world, tiny wants, the bliss of boredom, of desires so simple their unfulfillment could be a kind of pleasure too.

OF BLINKING AWAY THE SAME old bad news. The images of death came daily, sterile, dressed often in blue plastic gowns and nylon gloves. Another image was of a number, illustrated to show how it climbed. Then amid this dreary parade came one of a different type: you could watch a man die. Not dressed in the blue gown, not crowned by ventilator tubes, not behind the closed doors of quarantine, but in his own skin, on the street, his killer no mystery of disease but one of his own kind. You could press repeat, could resurrect the man and pause. The man on the screen, the corpse on the screen, the same screen where your grandmother's mouth spat out a loquat seed. Her body expelled a nameless need. She fled the screen and fled the house. Behind the shut door, the dog's bark was sharp with sudden loneliness. To the top of the high hill her legs went, and there she stood looking dumbly at the city at her feet, at the roofs of houses inside which persons had shut themselves, inside which bodies sat, alone, struck dumb by the reality of what could be seen. It occurred to her then that she was here. Part of the picture she looked at, even if at its very edge, and she always had been part of it, whether others saw her here or whether she saw herself. She could climb inside invisibility and wander the streets, watching, construing herself a pair of eyes with no skin in the game, so to speak. But *here* was a real place where her feet met the ground upon which they stood. She was here, here and nowhere else, for the rest of the season by mandate of public health, for the rest of her life by mandate of everything else. On the other side of the world the place where her feet might have met another earth had been firmly occupied by others. Too late to be anything but an American, so here she was, an American in America, warts and all. A door opened. Then, another. One by one bodies rose from the world of images and entered the street. Maybe it was the ecstasy of not knowing what the future might look like, of looking at the past with fresh bewilderment: she wanted to hold a person's hand. So windows opened, doors unlocked, and human place pulsed, a returning beast. So many feet wiped away the emptiness of yesterday's city.

MORE AND MORE, SHE WAS hearing her grandmother's voice. For years her family had been congregating, unbeknownst to her, in a room you could enter with a few taps on the screen of your phone. You could enter without your body, which was its present utility; inside she felt something like the dream of immortality. Messages seemed to scroll back infinitely. Photographs, videos, birthday and holiday wishes, long blocks of Chinese text she copied into a translation tool to read:

"The scans the hospital doctor say week after mother is stubborn perineurial cyst, wish to home recovery tomorrow she prefers"

"She possessing obdurate mind. Not can comprehend to persuade without contemporary rules of society"

It was a magic trick. To be so suddenly close to those whose relation to her had been defined by the combination of infrequency and intensity. Suddenly, small talk. Daily photos, articles on new health fads, lopsided laughing emojis, and a family favorite, the image of a single stemmed rose. In the evenings, mornings on the other side of the world, group calls she could join effortlessly, with a caress of the finger, and out came her grandmother's voice. Bored, irritated, childlike with impertinence; it said, "Why won't you come?" Then paused as if remembering something, and turned to the trees in the garden, the weeding, the pruning, the harvesting, going on rapidly in dialect. Her grandmother spoke now almost exclusively in dialect, as if to rebuke her wandering descendants. The woman understood every fourth or fifth word.

"Mawmaw, how's your health?" she said.

"My health, I'm healthy! You can come back already, the pomelos are almost ripe."

Lulu's voice told another story. In the middle of the night their grandmother had woken to use the toilet and walked off the edge of the stairs. She still remembered who she was, but had lost all knowledge and sense of space. In the streets where she had lived for all of her life she would be suddenly lost, as if transported to a foreign land. Her inner compass was smashed, Lulu explained. She could walk back and forth down the same block and think she had reached the market; she could walk for a mile into town believing she was circling her own walled garden. She was no longer allowed to leave the house alone. The doctor had prescribed a black band that snapped around her wrist, inside which was embedded a GPS tracker the size of a fingernail.

"I can push this button," her grandmother said, chuckling, "and wherever I am, Lulu will come and get me."

Basking in summer sun, fruits ripened. Everywhere, they stained the sidewalks purple and black with their fallen crop. Canopies of cherries, plums, and apricots dangled beyond the woman's reach. Green apples and hard figs that would soften, yet still hung too high on the branch. A bountiful orchard bloomed, announcing its citizens, each flaunting its life and sustenance. The woman was going mad with the sight. Did the neighbors not love fruit? She imagined waiting beneath trees with her mouth open, catching the ones that fell before they smashed into the concrete.

Under the loquat tree, the dog's nose sniffed. Happily she licked at the trampled peels. Normally the woman did not like the dog to eat from the ground, but at this she could cry with happiness. "Here," she said, pointing to a loquat that was only a little bruised. The dog came and ate, licking her black lips in pleasure, looking eagerly at the woman for another direction.

"I always said dogs had the best life in America."

She looked up and saw her grandmother.

Her grandmother was dressed for an outing, in black elastic pants and a patterned silk shirt. On her feet were the purple Nike sneakers the woman had brought on her last visit home, five years ago. She looked healthy. The skin on her cheeks was plump and glowing.

"Is that your little dog?" her grandmother said.

"Yes," the woman said.

"She's pretty," her grandmother said.

"Yes."

"I had a little dog once. Lulu begged for one, after her mother died. I felt sorry for her. She wasn't very nice to her mother. I took her to the village where the strays were always having babies, and we carried one home. In the beginning we were happy. That dog had brown spots. He loved to eat oranges. But none of us knew how to make a little dog live. It got sick and died. Lulu was distraught. She blamed me. She said, 'You wanted to teach me a lesson, you let my dog die.'"

On the screen her grandmother's hair had gleamed silver. Here it was white, and soft like snow. A bandage covered the back of her head where it had been injured from her fall.

"How did you get here?" the woman asked.

"How should I know?"

"Do you know where you are?"

"You're here, so I must be far from home."

The woman opened her mouth to speak and her grandmother stopped her.

"Don't worry," her grandmother said, pointing to her wrist. The black band with the GPS tracker was wrapped around it. "I've got this."

She wanted to embrace her grandmother. She could not remember if embracing was something they did. "It's good to see you," she said. "You look well."

"Is that your little dog?" her grandmother said.

Slowly the woman nodded.

"She's pretty," her grandmother said.

"She's clever too," the woman said carefully. "Look." She asked the dog to sit, to turn around, to jump in the air, and the dog did so, eyes sparkling with intelligence and pride.

"She's a good student, like you," her grandmother said. "I had a little dog once."

"Yes."

Then her grandmother reached up, and the loquat branch dipped to meet her hand. With ease she plucked two. She peeled off the skin in petals and left them haloing the fruit. Its pale flesh glistened in the sun. She offered one to her granddaughter. "They're very sweet," she said.

For a moment the woman hesitated. She did not know the last time she had been handed a peeled fruit like this, like a child. For a moment she hesitated, then she took it, and bit into the sweet flesh greedily, and the cold juice ran into her mouth.

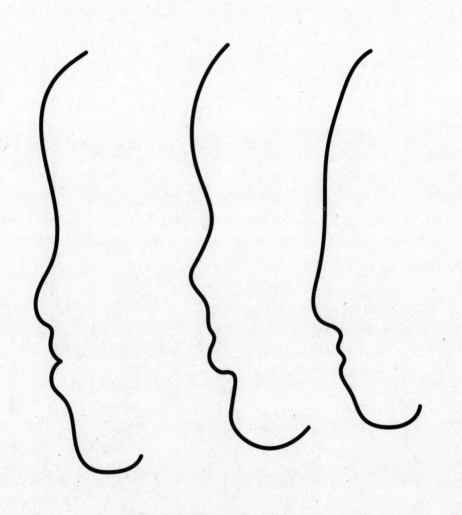

The Odd Women

VANDANA

Many would swear to what they saw. In the hours and days immediately following, they spoke of the incident compulsively, with the fervor of the evangelical:

"It was—"

"—*terrible*—"

"You could hear the train coming—"

"—and those gates, with the flashing lights,"

"Bells, horns, that horrible whistle—"

". . . I could hear it in my *skull* . . ."

"I saw her running from a block away and"

". . . wearing all black,"

"one of those jogging sweatshirts"

"—terrifying to witness. I wish . . ."

"—you couldn't see her face!"

"She must have been young, she moved so quickly—"

". . . people were shouting, I think I was too . . ."

"In that moment I really got what it means to *fear*, I mean, *really*—"

"I think I started *praying*—"

"—and then it was too late."

"*Praying! Me!*"

"it was so *loud*"

". . . and a hush came over everything, like a fucking blanket of silence."

"I couldn't hear myself think!"

"When the train stopped . . ."

"I just—blinked. Couldn't believe my eyes."

A door on the front train car opened. The conductor stepped out. On her face was a look of terror and wonderment. She walked to the front of the train, turned, and followed the track, peering with fright into the space beneath the wheels. She walked the full length of the train before turning toward the forming crowd with a knotted brow. Some peeled off to retrace her steps. Others spoke loudly on the frayed ends of excitement, or to hold off the failure of comprehension. Eventually investigators and responders arrived, followed by a smattering of news vans. Statements were taken; the crowd thinned. The passengers aboard were released and exited grumbling and confused. On the local evening news, the incident was given a five-minute segment: "At approximately ten after five this evening, a woman was seen by multiple eyewitnesses running headfirst into an oncoming train in District Eleven. After thorough investigation, no traces of a body could be found. Neither was the woman seen leaving the scene. At least seven confirmed bystanders claim to have witnessed the train hit a woman who looked like she was out for a jog. In an official statement, the conductor operating the train said that she saw a person jump in front of the train, after which she immediately engaged the emergency brake system. The train, apparently unmarked and unscathed, is currently being swiped for human traces, and a ground operation has commenced in search of the woman many are calling the ghost runner. Here now to speak with us is a local resident who was at the scene—"

URSULA

Nature had returned and thrived. In the yard, grass grew tall as girls, bent together and whispering, and where the blue blades parted, folding at their waists, blossoming weeds bobbed sweet smiling heads. Vines climbed over the cracked concrete frame and caressed the graffiti-sprayed walls. Through a shattered window on the ground floor, they saw the interior of the house, carpeted in wild orchids and mosses, under which the shapes of tables, chairs, beds, and even the metal frame of a reading lamp could still be traced. It was the perfect set for the film, presented like a beautifully packaged, ready-made gift: all they had to do was bring the equipment and shoot.

They walked across the grass, tamping a trail to the door. The lock broke easily. They entered into the dark floral smell, of earth and rain and nectar, and bowed their heads as they went through. A layer of soil had lifted the floor while branches, vines, and hanging moss lowered the ceiling. Like the tangle of a rain forest, dark as a cave. They walked through the rooms in silence, through the burgundy poppies carpeting the bedroom, the pink-and-white peonies in the study, to the bright kitchen blooming with yellow tulips and daffodils, none needing to voice the sacred feeling: *beauty!*

A crack—and the spell broke. Under the foot was not the expected snapped twig or root but instead a broken bone. Each living bouquet bloomed—in the shape of a body. At the roots: a shattered skull, two, three, eleven in total, maybe more. Sight became knowledge: they fled.

Soon investigators arrived. Questioning the neighbors provided little fruit, as most had known the place only in its current overgrown state. From pieces of testimony, only the barest of stories could be formed. Once a woman had lived here, reclusive and unremarkable, of whom little was known or seen. When the property began to fall into neglect, decades ago, it was assumed that she had moved away, though none remembered seeing her leave. Some remembered a period of disgust and disrepair, when the property emitted a rancid smell, and scavenging animals were spotted on the grounds, trailing clouds of flies—though it was possible this memory had been dislodged and enlivened by the recent discovery. Perhaps, in the neighborhood association, there was discussion of what to do with the property once it became an eyesore, but a matter had arisen with the lien that made pursuing it more trouble than it was worth. Over time the eyesore grew into its present state, and became a fixture, a wild park nobody entered from a vague inherited sense of fear.

At the laboratory, samples were analyzed. The initial suspicion that the mass death was related to the latest pathogen or political upheaval was soon dismissed: the corpses were over thirty years old. Further tests detailing genetic makeup seemed to indicate a mistake had been made. New investigators returned with oversight and a stricter set of protocols; new samples were collected and analyzed with supervision and exacting documentation. But when the tests were run again, the results were identical to the first. This process was repeated again, yielding again the same results; biologists and geneticists examined and reexamined them in amazement and disbelief. The genetic code from every separate corpse—thirteen total, it was finally determined—was not just similar but identical, down to the last nucleobase pair, a biological impossibility never before seen, even in cases of laboratory-engineered monozygotic twins. The perfect identity of genetic and epigenetic code, the perfect identity even of biological traces and residues of time and experience, was such that even the wild speculation of cloning had to be dismissed. Nonsensical as it was, the only accurate way to describe what had been found was this:

thirteen separate corpses of one person, born into the same body, living the same life, and dying the same death—by gunshot to the head.

OCTAVIA

For a week or two Mina had not heard from her mother, not a photo of the dog nor complaint that she never called, not even a text saying love you dear with a double heart icon, which her mother sent usually at least once every two days. She called and there was no answer. She sent a mirror-shot of her face on the messenger and waited for a response. Her mother lived alone on the other side of town, a forty-minute bus ride away. It was not recommended to visit your mother or to take buses in times like these unless you had no other choice; people looked at you and said, "Selfish."

The bus was empty. Every so often the driver's eyes regarded Mina in the rearview mirror with curiosity. The rest of the face was hidden behind a shield. Lockdowns had become routine in the past decade; sometimes the lines of transportation that connected people to others were chock-full and flowing, but when necessity called they emptied instantly, like a faucet that could be turned on and off. Mina wondered if the driver liked being surrounded by others or if she preferred to be alone. Mina tried to smile from behind her own shield. Forty minutes later she exited through the back doors, tossing a meek "Thank you" toward the front.

Her mother's car was in the driveway, but there was no answer at the door. Well, the dog barked. She could hear the dog pawing at the door, her untrimmed claws scratching and even turning the knob, but apparently it had been bolted shut. She waited and rang the bell again. Finally she heard footsteps, and a voice that did not sound like her mother's:

"Just leave it at the door!"

"Who are you?" Mina said.

A pause. Mina imagined the person looking through the peephole, examining her.

"What are you doing here?" the person said. "Go home."

"Who are you?" Mina said again. She ran through the list of people her mother might have let inside. A friend from painting group, a new health aide, neighbor Patty?

"Who are you?" Mina said a third time.

"It's me, bub. It's your mom."

"You don't sound like my mom." But her mother did call her bub.

"I'm—" A sigh. "The truth is I'm not doing so hot. I'm not—myself. Well. That's not quite right. I am myself. That's the problem."

"What the hell does that mean?" Surely her mother kept a spare key somewhere. Mina picked up an empty flowerpot, then another. She flipped over stones in the dirt beside the stoop, shook spiders from the cobwebbed bushes.

"Stop that," her mother said. "I'm going to let you in. Just—you should be prepared. I look—I don't look normal. Just promise me, okay? Promise me you're not going to freak out. None of this 'you don't sound like my mom' shit. It's me, okay? If you don't trust me, trust Abigail. Abby knows who I am. She's excited to see you."

Abby barked as if to say yes.

"Promise?"

"Okay."

The door unbolted and opened. Abby leaped out, mauling Mina with a wet tongue.

"Close the door."

Mina did.

The back of a person was moving down the hall. Abby followed, so Mina did too, though she did not recognize the person as her mother. She did not recognize the person as her mother but her eyes also did not say, "This is not my mother." They said, "This is not anyone." She could find no precedent of sense or language to describe it. It was as if she were looking at the template of a person, one of those featureless mannequins, except it was impossible to fix in sight, like an image in a dream. Not that the figure was transparent—the window behind it was blocked, and there was the shadow. But that her mother— yes, the more she looked, the more correct it felt to call it her mother—provided no visual data at all.

Her mother sat at the kitchen table and gestured for Mina to sit across from her. Abby curled up at her mother's feet. Her mother looked at her intently and Mina looked back. Tried. The face refused to be recognized. Was her mother thin? Pale? Mina didn't know. But there was malaise coming from the face, that was clear. Her mother was unwell.

"I guess this is what happens when I keep to myself," her mother said. "I never knew, though I should have. I guess I've always been careful. And you've been around. I feel pretty weak . . . depleted. Empty. I even"—she laughed heartily, like she was really telling a joke—"I thought about gulping a jar of pain milk. Who knows if that would have worked."

"Mom!"

"Yes?" Her mother's voice trembled. "Keep it coming. Keep looking at me. Talk to me. Tell me what's going on with you."

So Mina did, speaking of life with a partner, of the little arguments they'd recently had, having no one else with whom to diffuse their frustrations and moods. The recent lockdown had been announced just as they were planning to go traveling together; instead, they'd settled and rooted into their new home.

Sometimes they took long walks and saw more of the new neighborhood, which was beautiful; Mina hadn't noticed how lovely the gardens were, though perhaps they were better tended during these days. Her partner was talking about starting a garden herself, and had begun to forage for mushrooms in the nearby woods. "I've missed you," Mina said. How easy it was to talk to her mother about the mundanities of her life, the mundanities that could only be of interest to one's mother, the one woman on earth who just wanted you to be happy and well. As Mina spoke, her mother's face came into definition. The lines on her mother's hands, folded on the table between them, etched into the knuckles and hollows where Mina remembered them to be. Mina looked at the hands and seemed to conjure there with her sight the scar by the right thumb, burned when Mina was a child, her mother saving her from a bowl of hot soup she had carelessly picked up and immediately dropped. Now she began to recognize other features: the eyes, the chin, the crease beside the lip. After an hour of sitting and talking with her mother, sitting too close unshielded for health guidelines, the person finally looked again like her mother. Sick, yes, but her mother. Mina was confused, and relieved.

VANDANA

Immediately following the incident, the conductor was brought into the station to describe the face she had glimpsed for one moment before the train slammed into the body. Or failed to slam. The conductor had braced for the impact, muscles seizing, eyes, yes, closing, for at the last moment the runner had turned to face the train, the emergency brake had been pulled too late, it always was, and who wanted to watch a person die? But the impact never came. When the conductor opened her eyes a half second later, the person had disappeared as if into thin air.

The digitally reconstructed image of Vandana's face circulated for some days on local news and moved to the interfog of information and ideas, where it attracted a fair number of excited reactions and illuminations. But many exciting stories circulated in those days, stories whose explicit and implicit injustice and lines of infuriating causality could fuel you for many lifetimes. Across the continents and oceans, habitats of life were being irrevocably destroyed, while within the deteriorating biosphere new and ferocious diseases were brewing to counterattack humanity (the ardent voices of warning, for now, ignored), while within humanity ageless wars raged on, so where there was not overt war there was the climate of war, while within the remaining nation-states, spiraling galaxies of civil wars were waged against and by the powers that were. In other words: plenty to concern the attentive mind.

"Okay, weird. Next," noted one user below the image of Vandana's face, summarizing succinctly her story's public life.

Yet for some, the question remained. There were sightings:

"Didn't that girl look—"

"Have I seen you somewhere?"

"Is that—"

"Can't be,"

"No, I'm almost certain, she even had the—"

"Hey, you there, *wait!*"

Always Vandana was spotted turning a corner. By the time the same corner was turned by her pursuer, she had disappeared.

Deep in a noteroom, on a string dedicated to uncovering the secret of the ghost runner, a few dozen people mined potential sightings and theories several times a day. Wild and disparate theories, ranging from government conspiracies to speculations of magic and sorcery. There was a general consensus (as much as these rooms allowed) that only one such sighting was genuine. The text of the note, which had been illuminated hundreds of times, read:

> i was walking home from woofoods at 3ish and on the block up a head i saw some1 that was walking and i think they look familar but 4 a min cannot put my finger on it. preface i was there the day of the train OK so none of this facial reconstruction bs. i know what i saw. and then i realise that it was the person looked like THAT GRL. don't know how to explain it just smthing about the way she walked i guess. and then i realise shes wearing the same black hoody as the runner too. i should say i have clear-vid memory or whatever OK. so i start walking faster 2 catchup 2 her but not 2 fast that shed notice bc i dont want 2 scare her off. i guess id make a pretty good detective or pi because she didnot notice a thing and when i was close enough 2 grabher i blurt out HEY are you the ghost runner? and she turns and i imediatly know its her remember i have clearvid-memory. she looked v surprised. i know lotsofppl have stories like this 1 but if what happens next doesnt prove it is 4 real nuthing will. she looks like she was gonna run so i reach out andgrab her arm and what happened next was *my hand went right thru it like it was nothing there!!!* again *my hand went right thru her arm* like she didnt escape my grasp or smthing andshe didnt yank her arm away it was litrally like she was made of air or smthing i have never in my lifeexperienced something so freaky. by the time i realize whats happening ofc she was gone. like i said if this doesnt prove 2 u the govt is hiding topsecret shit like aliens and witches and the cure for ids nuthing will. stay vigilant, folx.

URSULA

How had the person/persons died? It looked like (mass) suicide. But for one significant detail: no weapon/weapons were found. The shot(s) to the head(s) had been made through the left temple(s) and impact pattern(s) appeared consistent with what would be expected from a self-inflicted gunshot wound. And yet if this were the case shouldn't the skeletons have been found each with a gun in or near the left hand? Where were the thirteen guns? The bullet casings were examined; it was discovered that they all came from the same (missing) gun, unless of course there existed a species of firearm similar to this species of person, that was singular and plural at once.

So maybe it was murder. Another person had come into this house and murdered the person/persons precisely to look like (mass) suicide. And yet there were no signs of struggle, in the body/bodies or on the property. An ordinary house had been excavated from beneath its jungle and was now an active investigative scene cordoned off by purple tape. Plant and animal samples were shipped to another facility for further study and analysis. Besides small leftovers of the now disbanded film crew, no traces of human DNA but the infuriatingly identical one/many. Furthermore, carbon testing determined that each body had begun its decomposition at more or less the same time. Either they had lined up to be killed or. Where were the thirteen murderers?

So it was suicide. The circle returned to its starting point but never closed.

Ursula's case was shelved, assigned to an archivist whose job was to make it look like the investigation was still ongoing. In fact the archivist was good at her job. She liked tending to these so-called cold cases, so-called cold because they lacked the drama of flaring climax and the tidy resolution that packed the originating questions away. Like life, she thought, these questions withheld answers. They could be kept alive and watched. Cold, no—some days the archivist thought of herself as the guardian of many small flames.

The archivist ran Ursula's genetic code/codes through a system that drew an estimation of the deceased woman's/women's face. Another person might have circulated these images publicly alongside a call for information. But the archivist shrank at the idea of putting a face into the wide world for scrutiny and recognition, even if its owner/owners were dead. Instead, she sat and looked at the face for some moments, as if saying hello to someone she'd known from long ago.

She erased the image and submitted an open-ended genetic match request. The woman/women must have had family, however distant, somewhere. This request ticked silently, eventlessly, in the background hum of the archive, gradually testing negative with each living known person in the datapond, and with the new sequences that trickled in daily. Years later, at the peak of a new pandemic, a yellow alert appeared on the screen.

The match was unusual. One core section of the genetic code was near identical, but it was not the section that usually corresponded to familial relationship. Rather, it was a part of what geneticists called the "white zone," whose function and expression were still unclear. In most humans this part of the code seemed to do nothing, an extraneous evolutionary remnant like the tailbone. The archivist opened the file. The person with the matching white zone code was an elderly woman, retired and divorced, with one child, living in this very city. But when the archivist went to examine the sequence, it began to change before her eyes. She blinked and leaned in. Soon an error alert blanked the letters—*Negative match: privacy breach*—and the file disappeared.

OCTAVIA

Two days and Mina's mother looked like her mother again. Mina registered her to test for the new virus. A strange virus, not just a variation of animal flus like those of years past; new cases showed that it was a kind of generalist, choosing in each host the weakest processes to interrupt, though how these were targeted was still a mystery. Was it possible that it could also attack something like the identity? When Mina considered where her mother was weak, identity came immediately to mind—after so much life, Octavia still did not know who she was. For years Octavia had identified herself as "mother" but then Mina left home and married, and Octavia's mother identity began to fray. Yes, the more Mina considered, the more certain she was: her mother had been losing her face for a long time.

Octavia distrusted hospitals; for years she had treated herself with home remedies, gingerroot and aniseed and turmeric stirred into tea. Octavia said hospitals made people sick: you went and caught one of the diseases housed there. Then you were snatched and kept, as in a prison, away from the general population.

When she saw the testing site, Octavia turned to leave.

"Come on," Mina said.

"Absolutely not."

"Do it for me. It can't hurt."

"What if it does?"

As Mina's mother resisted, she seemed to lose her features again. The lines on her face blurred. The pupils of her eyes diffused. Her hair wilted to an unstable cloud.

"Look, Mom, I'm worried about you. You don't look like yourself." Mina hugged her mom, firmly. She knew of her mother's fear of technology, how her mother refused to have her picture shot and hated appearing on vids. Octavia complained that she did not really know how to be with someone unless they were face-to-face. And people liked being face-to-face with Octavia; almost everyone her mother met felt before her a natural intimacy. Mina got the impulse, to an extent. During quarantines, she too missed the ease of human company unmediated by machines. What she could not understand, however, was the suspicion of modern medicine.

"Just let me be a good daughter for once, okay?"

Mina looked at her mother with tenderness. She looked at her mother with the desire for her own peace of mind. As she looked, resignation and duty softened her mother's brow. Her mother nodded, looking more like her mother again. They walked into the site.

A small vial of Octavia's blood was sent to the laboratory for sequencing.

The test, a near instant procedure involving a biological mirror, reflected the virus and sample off each other to determine identity or lack thereof. Initially the vial containing Octavia's sample reflected negative; the result was logged by a small artificial memory and dumped into a cistern of data. But between the initial moment of reflection and the completion of the test, Octavia's sample transformed. When the final result was delivered to human eyes, prompting crumpled brows and questioning clicks, it could only be attributed to error, likely human. Somebody had contaminated the sample, or lost it, the careless technician who'd collected it, the careless courier who'd delivered it, the careless technician who'd unpacked and loaded it into the machine. How else could such a result be explained, perfect identity with the virus, a 100 percent match, a nonsensical result insinuating that the subject was the virus itself?

The subject was contacted and a message was left, professing apologies and requesting a return to redo the test, but they did not hear from Octavia again.

VANDANA

The word had entered her vocabulary with a dull recognition, even as she knew it was missing something. Superpower, Vandana thought, is that what I have? There was something juvenile about it, a sort of gung-ho jubilation that made her want to curl into her sagging couch with a tub of melting ice cream.

For as long as she could remember she had drifted in and out of materiality. She had not thought it strange. Some people could run far and fast, some could play the violin, some could speak in numbers as if they were words. Vandana could make herself immaterial. "You know, I can walk through walls," she joked to a lover once. All it required was a certain peace of mind. Though she sometimes thought of it as a talent, a special ability, most days it was just a part of her temperament, like her love of strawberry syrup, or her arousal in total darkness, unremarkable and private.

She showed her lover. She turned Louise to the mirror and stepped into her body. Louise let out a noise somewhere between a laugh and a scream. But she did not flee in fear, and Vandana basked in happy shock.

"You should use this thing," Louise said. "I mean, fuck. Think of what you could do. All the *good* you could do!"

"Good? The good I could do—yes!" Vandana laughed. She was young and full of hope. She wanted to do good, to *be* good: she wanted Louise to think she was good. She enrolled in boxing classes. She trained her body. Naturally clumsy, small, and un-athletic, she nevertheless won whenever she practiced fighting with Louise. How could you defeat an opponent you couldn't touch? She drank in the amazement on Louise's face, the amazement that was hungry and wild. When she made her body solid again it was positively vibrating.

So this was love: Vandana ecstatic with purpose. As a child she had stumbled into these states without knowing how; now she sharpened her awareness, her sensitivity, and entered them according to her desire and mood. She trained her power. Her mind blank, her lungs open, she recognized the body as a co-incidence. Just an arrangement of atoms, like anything else. Air became her, and so did the wall or the earth or another being—Louise—whatever she encountered, another coincidence that might be momentarily rearranged. The world did not lose its beauty. No, it was sublime. Vandana moved through the atomic field awed by the absence of particularity. Like a child she played inside immateriality, delighting, throwing handfuls of sand in the air. With her lover she learned to tease. Put your hand here, then disappear. Your mouth there. Take your tongue away, then appear it, slowly, inside of her.

When her body was spent, she gave her mind to Louise's scheme, embarking on a cultural education, gulping down stories of mutants and weirdos rising into their moral glory. In these stories there was always the reckoning with the burden, the reckoning with fear. To overcome fear of danger and fear of responsibility required courage, and a certain gumption. Gumption, which a person like Louise seemed to possess in spades. Vandana wanted Louise to teach her how to muster this gumption.

She began to stalk the streets at night, eyes peeled for evil. And discovered that evil was not so easy to recognize as in the vids. Whenever you saw someone doing something that might look that way on the glittering screen you looked into their eyes and saw they were just trying to live their life. Vandana felt an intruder in another's privacy. Sometimes, she felt an intruder in her own. The difficulty, the difficulty, she said to Louise. She tried to tell Louise that doing good was difficult because evil seemed always to be wrapped up in costumes or hidden behind closed doors. "But you can walk through those," Louise said, impatient. Louise's gumption: she got a little bored. Vandana walked through Louise's closed doors and found her with another lover, brazenly, knowing Vandana's ability, as if begging to be discovered and released.

Swiftly the pointed arrow of purpose flew from her. In the stories Louise had shown Vandana, love was always an obstacle to be overcome. Sometimes the lover died, renewing the glorious weirdo with tragedy. For righteous revenge the heroines fought; with righteous solitude they pushed loved ones away to keep them safe. But where was the loneliness, tucked somewhere between the spandex cape and the denouement? Where was the doubt? Not just the plot device of doubt but doubt like the doubt of god.

Loveless, godless, Vandana clung to the shadow of Louise, and the call to use her power for good. She turned to pure reason and walked its mazes with a lonely, calculating eye. She saw a hopeless world, in which the worst of civilization no longer wielded their weapons at the surface but rather embedded them deep within the rules of governance, the rules of the market, and the rules of law, dressed in the lovely sheens of prosperity, well-being, and peace between ruling bodies. Theoretically Vandana could seek the ruptures of the sheen, place herself against the powers that were, in overregulated communities and so-called danger zones. Or she could seek the unwanted tasks that materiality made dangerous. She could use her ability stealthily, work against the governing bodies using their own tactics, knowing she could never be imprisoned. She could, she could. She walked the maze of reason until her mind buzzed blank.

Once she'd been let in on a secret. Now she was barging in.

URSULA

To imagine, she had laughed the first time. Oh, *how* she had laughed! Guffawing, slapping her knee. Ursula and Ursula, cackling on their backs like a couple of hyenas, with the glee of what they'd discovered.

A simple problem had started it. A party: Ursula wanted to go and Ursula didn't want to go. Ursula could see herself, leaning against the bar, sipping gin from a plastic cup. She would lean into a stranger's life and say, "Is it glamorous? Tell me it's glamorous," and leave the print of her black lipstick on the plastic rim. But Ursula preferred to stay home in her pajamas and drink a vid about a fake person's glamorous life. Ursula wished not to have to look in the mirror, to wonder, am I wearing the right thing am I saying the right thing am I too drunk too sober not enough of either to be interesting why is it so incredibly loud when I breathe.

"If only I could cut me out, like a psychological surgery," said Ursula.

"Yes, I'd leave the nag behind," replied Ursula, "and save her for when she's useful."

Their wishes were granted. Ursula was in bed in her pajamas, hiding under the covers, reciting her little worries and chewing her little nails. Ursula was in bed and Ursula also stood before the bathroom mirror, preening in the white light. Ursula and Ursula, giggling with disbelief. Ursula was very comfortable on her bed and could imagine lying curled there forever. Ursula swiped black paint over her lips, already starting to feel beautiful, to feel like a dark, sweet beckoning, to be devoured in one untarnished bite.

The second time, heartbreak was the cause. "You want," said the one who'd sipped from the black-rimmed cup, "something I'm unable to give." Ursula denied wanting but was unconvincing; Ursula wanted everything. Most of all she wanted to kill her loneliness, which was worse when you remembered being warmly held. To divide herself was a necessity. Broken Ursula, weeping endlessly, drowning in self-pity. She was a tumor! "Excise her," said the Ursula who wanted to party, and she did.

It became useful again and again to leave a version of herself behind. She—they—didn't really understand it, but they were comforted—thrilled—intrigued by the ability to present one consistent face to the world while the questioning and bickering others remained hidden, each one a secret weapon in her arsenal of selves. Well, the world positively demanded the division of the self! It was a great comfort—thrill—intrigue—pleasure— logical solution for every Ursula to be queen of her own place and situation. To know one's characteristic so indisputably and to inhabit it: a fine way to live. Even sorrow, if it was all you had to attend to, could be a pretty thing to turn and look at in different lights.

When they realized the magic worked only one way it was too late. The house was awfully small. Money was a problem. According to the government, which governed reality, only one Ursula had real-ly been born, so only one Ursula could real-ly work. The reasoning Ursula set ground rules. They could leave the house two at a time—doubles didn't turn too many heads—but never more than two. For most errands they sent the unassuming Ursula, who dispatched tasks quickly and efficiently, and did not draw attention to the fact that she was shopping for a dozen. But only a few of the Ursulas actually liked hiding. Even the Ursula who loved to cook and clean got tired of cooking and cleaning for so many. And then there were the fights, about horribly little things:

"Of course I should go, I am the clever one," said Ursula.

"But you've got *zero* charisma," replied Ursula.

And Ursula would come in, waving her hands with conciliatory hope: "How about me? They'll like me, I'll make them all feel comfortable and happy, and—"

Somebody screamed.

The scream of a final Ursula being born. The Ursula who needed to get out. Out of the house, away from the incessant noise, away from the bickering, fighting, competing, calculating, considering, constantly weighing this-one-or-that-one selves. What had started as a joke was now like being drawn and quartered, a mare tied to each limb and galloping everywhere. It was useful to fracture yourself, but what happened when you wanted again to be whole? And how was it possible to still feel so lonely in a house full of bodies? Ursula surveyed this tormented scene and walked out the door.

The sun was shining, people were out, a breeze lifted Ursula's feet. She walked away from the house of her selves and with each step she was lighter. She walked past strangers, toward the busy blocks of the neighborhood where people shopped and sat on the sidewalks eating ice cream with their lovers. How she missed the presence of other people—souls that vibrated with life but who were opaque to her, to whom she could be mysterious as well. Even to a friend, you weren't known like you knew yourself. Like you knew your own ugliness. Ursula walked without thinking where she was going, only knowing it was away from those souls who knew her too well. It was nearly dusk before she realized she was headed in the direction of a friend.

Would this friend recognize the newest Ursula? Ursula had known Octavia since childhood—even in the children's home, the home for misfits and loners, they had been different together. Octavia was the special kind of soul who might see your ugly and still love you. But some weeks ago, lonely Ursula had invited Octavia to her house, daring to show the truth of herself to another for the first time. When she opened the door to all of her selves, Octavia had frozen.

Now this Ursula wanted to meet Octavia. To seek her exquisite compassion, or to test it? Ursula, walking to clear the noise in her head, found her head filled suddenly with clanging and ringing. She had reached the tracks and a train was coming. The flashing gate came down before her.

She blinked. The people around her were gesticulating and shouting. She turned her head and saw:

a figure flying toward the tracks. Accelerating at a significant rate, clever Ursula might have noted, and charted the collision course in her head. Kind Ursula would have thrown her own body before the train to force the other out of the way. Together, the brains and heart might even save the reckless stranger. This Ursula stared. She was graceful, the running girl. Fast, but not desperate, no, she moved with joyful inevitability. At the moment of encounter—the woman suspended, like a jellyfish in the sea, the train creaking and screaming to a halt—a cold wind rushed into Ursula's mouth, cleansing her body, and she felt—what *was* this feeling—

Freedom? Or the ghost of it, the hope?

OCTAVIA

For most of her life Octavia had feared being alone and avoided it at all costs. She'd surrounded herself with people, built a veritable world out of others. She had been an addict of human company, like her ex-wife had once been of drink. But now:

"Mina, Mina," she said, hugging her grown girl's arms. "You can't watch over me forever, can you?" She sent her daughter home.

Gingerly, like an old woman taking a wobbly seat, like the old woman Octavia now was, she slid back into being nobody.

Literally. Horribly. For as long as she could remember, Octavia had taken shape and form as a mirror did, perfectly reflecting the person you needed her to be. Her body did this independent of her will or desire, like a magnet moving toward its pole. First the tug, and then she was snapped into being. She had not been wholly conscious of it until Mina's birth, when realization smacked her in the face. The total transformation of her body into "mother" was sudden and lasting. Her hips widened, her flat breasts swelled, her thin arms grew sturdy and strong. Her eyes changed into eyes that saw danger everywhere. Her heart changed into a heart that cared about the happiness of her child over the happiness of any other.

Even after her nature became clear, Octavia could not prevent it. Her face morphed. The timbre of her voice rounded or thinned. Her body moved and her brain reacted—mysteries and surprises that depended on who was looking. Intuitively her body enacted the other's wants.

It was not a curse. Octavia had loved her nature, and embraced it as a gift. Without meaning to she had honed and directed this . . . *ability*, to create the community she'd never had growing up. In the children's home, she had dreamed of a little house bursting with family, on a street where every person you met was a new or old friend. Octavia's world. Oh, it *was* wonderful to be perfectly beloved. For a while she had lived in a safe little sac of need, cushioned by others who would never leave because they depended on her. When she'd met the girl who could make her dream true, who had a big, loud family that still lived on the street where she grew up, it had been so easy to make that girl love her back. And how thrilling, to become another's dream! "Everything I could have asked for and more," Octavia's wife had said, feeling the cliché in her bones.

But eventually the spell wore off. Or was it Octavia who couldn't wear the costume of someone else's desire forever? Whose fault was it, then, that her love wanted suddenly an ugly wife, a mean wife, a petty wife who gave her every excuse she desired to leave?

Then Mina had grown up and left home too.

Now Octavia met isolation as a long-lost sibling. In the past decade, with mandated curfews and quarantines unpredictable as weather, she had acquired little tastes of loneliness. Like her first tastes of fine wine, they had initially repulsed her. No, more like a pungent fruit or bitter vegetable: to enjoy loneliness properly required a sophisticated palette and a pinch of daring. Octavia was becoming sophisticated in loneliness. Initially she'd tempered her tastes, planning excursions after long stretches alone, going to the store or to see a friend on their patio, just as she was beginning to lose her shape. Carefully she'd dosed herself in isolation. But in the most recent lockdown, she'd gone farther than ever before.

Mina had come and saved her, just when she was on the verge.

"You don't look like yourself," Mina had said. Octavia had heard this line before. There had been brief moments when her terrible subjectivity flared through before she could suppress it, and anyone who caught a glimpse of her face made this same irritating comment. "You don't look like yourself." How did they know what she looked like, when she herself had no idea?

Alone again, she melted daringly, sweetly, back into her nothing. The little particles of Octavia drifted off without the glue of identity, floating loosely in a human shape. She was disintegrating. She was reaching for a feeling—no, the memory of a feeling, from when she was younger than Mina was now. From when she hadn't yet made the decisions that led to the life she now lived.

She had been fresh out of university. She had recently moved to the city, encouraged by a childhood friend who'd lured her with the promise of limitless possibility. More than a friend—Ursula was like an older sister. Both had been left by their birth mothers at the home as infants; neither had walked out until she was an adult. Though Ursula had always said, defiantly, that she didn't like any of the prospective new mothers, Octavia knew the truth. Ursula had stayed to look out for her. Ursula had worried that Octavia was too weak, too easily manipulated, too kind, and became strong and hard enough for the two of them combined. In some ways, Ursula had understood Octavia's nature before she had herself.

With Ursula and Ursula alone, Octavia had sometimes felt the pull of the magnet and decided to break in the other direction. Sometimes.

But Ursula had changed in the time they'd spent apart. Perhaps it was the city; perhaps it was age; each time Octavia saw her, Ursula seemed to be someone else. Octavia could not put her finger on her friend. In adult Ursula's presence, Octavia was surprised to find herself flattened and thin; before Ursula she felt not as if coming home to an old self but rather jerked into shifting unexpected shapes.

One day, Ursula told her the reason: showed her. She warned Octavia not to be afraid. "Afraid?" Octavia dismissed, knowing that Ursula wanted her not to be, and flung open the door of Ursula's house. She looked at Ursula and at the other Ursulas looking at her. How could I not be? she thought. She had needed no explanation, though one of the Ursulas was happily answering every question she did not ask.

Standing before all of them, Octavia had felt herself spreading, like light, into a state of calm fluidity, peacefully inhabiting all her possibilities at once. For the first time in her life, she felt no urgency to fix herself into one. Ursula was not just one either. Perhaps Ursula felt it too, the confirmation that they'd always possessed something secret and shared. Ursula was trying to explain how she had become this way, Ursula was saying something important. Octavia was lost in her own feeling.

"You look funny," Ursula told her.

"I feel funny," Octavia said.

Some weeks later, Ursula had burst through Octavia's door. Just one of her, Octavia had no idea which. Ursula's face wild with windblown surprise, and a stone-cold ecstatic look in her eyes. "I know exactly what to do," she'd announced. "To solve my problem."

"Your problem?" Octavia had felt herself growing bitter and defensive. It was always strange and a little invigorating to discover that the person you faced needed you to be mean.

Ursula looked at her. Sharp eyes. Hard, cold smile. "I thought you would understand. It's torture. I'm split into bits all the time, it's an impossible way to live."

Octavia shook her head. Ursula said she wanted Octavia to understand but really she wanted Octavia to confirm her conviction that she was incurably alone.

"Don't you know how good you have it?" Octavia had said. "You get to choose. The world is your fucking oyster." Octavia felt herself pointed in the direction of jealousy and she didn't mind going there. She was jealous. She didn't yet understand why, she couldn't yet say, "It's rude to complain about having too many selves to someone who doesn't have any." She mirrored Ursula's cold, sharp look. "You know, some people would kill for just one of you."

"Exactly," Ursula said.

If Octavia had known that would be the last time she would see her friend, would she have acted differently? If only all the Ursulas had confronted her, together. But that would never happen again. Never again would Octavia stand before another's full multiplicity, with the terror of free will on her tongue.

Alone, she inched toward that feeling. It was painful, unbearable, to not have another against which to orient herself. It was also the closest she felt to free. Octavia thought she finally understood that look in Ursula's eyes. She walked to the sweet-bitter edge where pain tumbled childlike into pleasure. What if she crossed it, what if she let herself dissolve?

VANDANA

One morning Vandana walked forward and the wall met her, solid as hell. She was confused. She tried again; again the wall refused. A bitter voice inside her laughed: "You longed to be ordinary, and now you are."

Her laugh flew out of her mouth. She was giddy. She was ready to prove the bitter part wrong, to say "I am ordinary!" happily. She caressed the boundaries of things, and her own. The wall, the door, the knob. She walked through empty space and felt the air brush the hair on her arms. She went into crowds of people and felt their heat, their shoulders bumping into hers. She ran into someone and nearly got into a fight, and oh, it was thrilling, the possibility that she could actually be hurt. She stored the thrill of those moments like fuel that would power her new self.

Some days Vandana felt free. To put your head down and just consider your own two feet! A sort of eternal childhood.

So where did the weight come from? When the high wore off, Vandana was exhausted and sore. She woke in the mornings assaulted by her solidity. Her body was heavy. The air was crushing. The light slanting through her window pinned her down.

Without her ability—her temperament—who was she? She had been tormented by the question of what to do with her ability, but without it, "Vandana" lost its shape, like an ice cube melted into a puddle on the floor.

Some days she found herself on Louise's street, walking up the steps to her ex-lover's door. She pushed her hands against the solid wood. If she pressed her finger into the doorbell, it would ring instead of going through. "I'm a different person now," she imagined herself saying. Then Louise opened the door and stared. By the look on her face Vandana knew. It had never been Vandana whom Louise had desired but her weirdness, the exotic lure of her power. Vandana turned and ran down the street, ran and kept running until her legs buckled beneath her.

She gasped. Doubled over and struggling to breathe—but somehow, she felt light again. In this way Vandana discovered she could banish the heaviness temporarily. No matter that it eventually returned. On good days she got out of bed and made herself run until the exploding hurt in her legs, her feet, her lungs, matched the emptiness pounding inside her. She ran until she could no longer hear the question of herself, until she was nothing more—nothing less—than her body.

She had not intended to cause a scene. She was not thinking of suicide. When she saw the train, it did not occur to her to ask her legs to stop. Blind in self-absorption, she did not see the people waiting patiently for the train to pass and did not hear their warning shouts. Senseless to everything but the strength in her legs, the blood swelling her muscles, the pain edging into her lungs, Vandana ran. In the moment the impact should have come, she thought, "I could die. Or I could live," and gave the answer to mystery.

When she returned to her solid body, she was inside a small room. Panting. She gulped a lungful of acrid air. It tasted of urine and sharp bleach. The room was a toilet—the closet-toilet of the train. She flipped up the lid and puked.

She looked at her face in the mirror. For a moment she held her breath. Then she moved her hand through her face, and laughed in relief.

Through the pocket window she saw the ambulance, the fire truck, the newsmobiles unpacking equipment, and the gathering chattering crowd. In the center of the crowd one woman stood frozen behind the flashing gate, staring right at her. For a moment Vandana stared back. The woman's face was ecstatic, ferocious, alive with a determination that made Vandana feel she could be anything, or nothing—either would be okay. She shook herself. She took off her sweatshirt and tied it around her waist. She washed her face. She rinsed her mouth. She let down her hair and wiped the sweat from her neck. Again she looked out the window at the staring woman. "What do I do now?" she asked. The answer came easily. She opened the door and let herself out. She filed off the train with the rest of the passengers onto a waiting bus, and rode it to wherever it was going.

URSULA

Death was no great equalizer. Thirteen times she died and not once was it the same as the last. Once, only, was there a moment of peace. The version of herself that had lived in a kind of happy resignation. Ursula killed that one first, to convince herself that what she was doing wasn't too cruel. That first death was like walking into a white light, almost as joyful as being alive. Immediately she realized it was a mistake. The worrier should have gone first, or the melancholic, prone to hysterics as they were. She shot them next, existing in a momentary hell of abject fear, then madness, total surrender to the unraveling. Then in the place of fear and madness there was nothing. They were dead.

She was disgusted with herself. A more vile creature had never walked the earth. She turned to her moral center, the one who saw her for exactly what she was. "You, of all of us," she said, cradling her head in her hand, "have made it hardest to live." She died with injustice on her lips. She closed that corpse's eyes.

"I'm ready," said the dutiful one, who was often the most courageous too. As she went, she felt the desire to keep living, like an apple bottled in the throat. It brimmed to her mouth and disappeared.

Her practicality's last thought was of the documents and money she would need, to leave this life and enter another undiscovered.

Her hope reached forward, riding an imagined future freedom into the burst of nothing. A climax whose zenith was   .

A soft hand took her wrist. "I can't take it anymore," her kindness said, and led her to the bathroom, where the remaining Ursulas would not have to watch. Her death was tender and yellow. Then her desire called, with a pained mixture of longing and regret, for the adventure of death and for all she had not yet seen. She turned to the joker next, whose laugh had grown unbearable. Into the final moment the laughter rang, meaningless as air, winking, nearly crying, as if it were all a game. When the laughter died she heard the snarl. Bitterness was easy to kill. She spat at herself, at the fate she had been handed, the fate she had endured—and all for what? A swift blow to her cursed head.

The one who lived in the past thought sweetly of the early days. Even before she was many, Ursula had been so capable— even as a child. Proudly independent, she'd believed she could do and be everything. How happy she had been, how happy they had been, to define and separate those capabilities into distinct entities, one to confront each aspect of the divided, complicated world. Now that world looked lovingly simple.

"Will it be too difficult to know who I am, without you?" she asked.

"And how has self-knowledge served us?" She was struck by wave upon wave of grief. "When it comes to living, I'm possibly more useless even than our morality. And you got rid of her so easily." She meant it as a comfort, not as a rebuke. Once nostalgia was gone, grief became a fact like any other.

Finally she sat down at the desk, across from her reason.

"Aren't you going to convince me to spare you?" she said.

"Aren't you hoping I will?"

Ursula turned the gun over in her hand. "Just say it," she said. "*It'll be useful to have me. Think of what we could accomplish together. None of the others to hinder us. You've always relied on me to survive. How will you do it without me?*"

"I did think of that. I can be wrong, you know. Once I theorized we were an evolutionary inevitability, an advancement of the species. A more complex and entangled selfhood to suit a more complex and entangled social ecology. It's possible I'm to blame for it all."

"And yet you are capable of revising yourself."

"I thought that was a gift once too."

"I don't see how it can hurt."

She looked across the desk into the penetrating gaze. She mourned her kindness now, who might have taken her hand and told a gentle lie.

"You are afraid you will be lonely."

She considered the gun in her hand. It was not too late to choose another path. Here she stood at the final fork in her road, and the possibility of more than one path was a comfort. The possibilities, plural, and her reason's ability to think down each one, to the future forks and the future forks, conjuring an infinity of could-be's. A comfort and a hope—reason had always seduced her with infinity. Reason took her hand and moved it away from her own head. "Weren't we always lonely? No escaping that." Reason brought the gun to herself, closed Ursula's hand around hers. "It's the only way. You'll see when it's done," she said. "You can do this," she said. She could. For as long as she'd existed Ursula had wondered who she was exactly in the congregation of her selves, the manifold whose identities and allegiances had been so clear. And she, blank, facing her reflections with bewildered calm. Now she was realizing. She was the one who would do anything to survive. She would survive. She pulled the trigger. The network of paths proliferated, with blinding speed, then in a flash there was only one. Singular—as she was now. The clarity! The horror. She stood up, and stepped forward onto the only road.

OCTAVIA

The doorbell rang.

Who was she going to be now?

Not a mother, nor a neighbor, nor even a patient. A stranger. Through the peephole Octavia saw a woman, late middle-aged, standing patiently. There was something off about her. Creepy. No—not the person. Behind her the sky was dark red.

Startled, she opened the door. "Good morning?"

"Good morning, hello!" said the visitor. "We don't know one another. I'm from the investigations department. Well, that sounds serious. I'm only an archivist. And I'm here in a personal capacity. A rogue agent, you might say." She laughed nervously.

"I've been looking for you. I mean, I discovered you by accident. I was working on another case, and—well, what I found made me want to meet you! On a totally unofficial basis, of course." A pause. "May I come in? I'm not infected."

She showed the screen that read *confirmed negative* in bright green letters.

"Better not, I haven't gotten tested," Octavia said. "And my daughter thinks I'm sick." For a moment she stood there staring at the sky. Like she had opened her door to Mars. Her curtains had been drawn all morning. It was 10 A.M., the sun should have been blazing straight into her eyes. Instead, she blinked into an eerie evening light. The streetlights still burned, and across the street, house windows glowed blue. No bird chatter. No wonder Abby was still asleep on her bed.

She turned her attention to the visitor. Suddenly dread climbed into her mouth, her cheeks, between her teeth. Dark red dread. Like death was riding swiftly her way. She slammed the door shut.

The visitor walked through the door.

Her body appeared, solid, first a hand and a nose, then the rest of her, fluidly, as if the door were not there. Of course the door was still there. Shut.

The visitor—the intruder—stood in the living room an inch from Octavia's face. From the hallway Abby appeared and sauntered over to her, sniffing. Abby sat and licked the intruder's hand.

"I don't mean to be rude," the intruder said. "You should know I don't just walk into anyone's house."

Octavia crinkled her eyes. The red sky, then this. How frightening, she thought. Strangely, she was not afraid.

"Okay," Octavia said. "Please, um, sit?"

The intruder sat, eagerly, shifting in her seat.

"Why the hell are you looking for me?" Octavia said after a pause.

"Because—" The intruder took a breath. "Because I think we are the same. Or similar."

Octavia raised her eyebrows. "I can't do that," she said. "I can't walk through things."

"But you can do something else?"

Octavia did not respond.

"I'm Vandana," the intruder said.

Octavia crossed her arms. "Octavia."

"Octavia, you don't know how thrilled I am to meet you. I should apologize. I don't just show people who I am. I've worked in the investigations department for oh, thirty years? I mostly work alone. I don't go out much. Folks look at me and see 'city bureaucrat'—which is exactly what I am! I'm that person they throw the cold cases to, to keep them just north of freezing. It's a great place to hide. I love it, really. I have plenty of time to think. And in all these years I've been monitoring these cold cases . . ." Vandana's eyes flashed. "I think I've been looking for something. In spite of myself." She gulped. She smiled sheepishly. "I've been looking for other people like me."

Octavia regarded Vandana now with curiosity. Octavia regarded herself. She felt, strangely, in the presence of someone she once knew. She felt strangely, yes. She did not understand it, her present state, but it was familiar. She had not yet fixed into anything. She had not yet oriented in the direction of Vandana's desire. She could not even feel that magnet in the distance toward which her body would inevitably transform. No, she was just as fluid as she had been before Vandana walked through her door. But without the unbearable looseness. A sort of ease. Strange. She looked at Abby, curled happily at Vandana's feet and already fast asleep.

"I can't walk through things," Octavia repeated.

Vandana smiled. "I guess that would be too easy."

"But I am—" Octavia narrowed her eyes. "Oh hell, why not? I'm like a mirror. I change depending on who's looking at me. You could say—you could say I'm highly adaptable. Usually."

"Usually?"

"I don't understand who you want me to be."

Vandana said, "Yourself, I guess."

Herself? Suddenly Octavia placed this sensation. She had been trying to reach this exact feeling, yet when it arrived, she'd nearly failed to recognize it. She squinted at Vandana, blinking. Blinking away the vision of Ursula and Ursula and Ursula, overfilling the room, relaxing Octavia into a calm state of possibility. None of them looking at her nothingness with fear, as even her own daughter had. Octavia's heart was in her throat. "Can you tell me what I look like?" she asked Vandana.

"What you look like?"

"Yes."

"Okay." Vandana leaned forward shyly. Vandana was her mirror; Vandana was heart-throated too. She looked at Octavia with concentration. "You have eyes. Um. You have a nose, and a mouth?" Vandana laughed. "You have a face! But I can't describe it much beyond that. It's hard to determine even the color of your skin, or eyes, or hair. They seem to be—shifting? You don't look like me, for sure. But it isn't alarming. I didn't even notice it until you asked."

"That's what I see when I look in a mirror." Octavia wiped her forehead. "I can't describe myself either. Or recognize myself. I can't look at myself and say, 'That's me!' Other people usually know exactly who I am, it's just me who has trouble. You know, I can't be photographed. Something happens to the image. I'm always turning my head, or blurred. I refuse now to be photographed, on principle, so nobody gets suspicious."

Vandana looked at her in awe.

"Can you control it? I mean, could you use it for something, if you wanted to?"

Octavia burst out laughing. "Are you here to convince me to join some end-of-the-world justice league?"

"Oh, no!" Vandana said. "God no. I only asked because—I *did* flirt with using my thing. When I was much younger—well. Maybe in another era I could have, I don't know, been a warrior goddess. But these days it's too complicated, isn't it? And my ability is quite useless against viruses, biological or technological. Yours probably is too. No, I was just curious." Vandana laughed: "I was lonely." She gave another hesitant smile.

Octavia didn't smile back like a good mirror. Suddenly she wished Vandana would stop looking at her, and stop saying things like "We are the same." She looked away. Through a crack in the curtains she saw the red that made everything feel unreal. "What's with the sky, anyway?" she said.

"No idea."

"I thought the world was finally ending. Then when you walked right in, I thought, This freaky lady is trying to recruit me. Too many old vids, probably."

Vandana said, "Oh, maybe the first part is true. I was drinking this vid the other day"—she scooted to the edge of her seat—"about the end, like the *end* end, of the entire universe. This scientist was explaining how the most likely scenario would be long and boring, because the universe was expanding, and . . ."

There was something sweet about the way Vandana spoke about the end of everything, with cheerful curiosity, her voice like a bird's song. Octavia tumbled into the stranger's song, walking through her speech like she was walking through her own thoughts. Even when the sky was blue it was green, Octavia thought. That was how she was starting to feel. Like if she were brave enough she would stand on her rooftop and shout, "The sky is green!" to whoever the fuck would listen. Instead, she imagined toward the end of her own self. Expanding, like the universe, at an accelerated rate. Baked into the preconditions of her. The birth of Octavia had been the birth of many potentials, running toward their solid states. Running until they broke loose. When would we know we were over the edge? Galaxies would unravel, planets and stars and pieces of space junk would be flung from the unraveling, settling gradually into ever-increasing solitudes.

"... not very dramatic, unfortunately," Vandana was saying. "Even black holes will be so far from anything that they'll just start eating themselves up, and—get this—*evaporating.*"

As girls, Octavia and Ursula had passed the time playing the multiverse like others played house. They'd open a portal and step into different lives. Ursula had played the role of anthropologist, noting observations about their imaginary destinations with distanced precision: "On this planet there are humanoid creatures similar to women but with more aggressive, violent tendencies, arising from a total lack of control over their means of reproduction," or "In this world, social order is determined by arbitrary characteristics such as color of skin and eyes," or "Here we encounter a people for whom the concept of 'I' does not exist." Sometimes these universes were so convincing that Octavia wanted to stay there. Perhaps this was why she'd struggled so to find herself in this life: she was waiting to discover a wholly different place, to encounter and embrace beings beyond her imagination.

"Did you ever find them?" Octavia said. "More people like you?"

"You mean, besides you? Perhaps. I have a couple of leads. One of them led me to you."

Octavia closed her eyes. "I had a friend," she said, "who was like you—like us. You would have liked to meet her, I think."

"Had?"

"I was jealous of her. She had so many selves, and I had none."

"She had many selves?" Vandana sat up. Octavia didn't notice, she was swimming in the sudden clarity of her memory.

"You wouldn't believe it unless you saw it. Ten or fifteen of her, the exact same person."

Octavia envisioned her Ursulas filling up the room.

"Where is she now?" she heard Vandana say.

"No idea. The last time I saw her . . ." She opened her eyes and looked at Vandana. "I think she was coming to me for help. I failed her. I never saw her again."

Vandana was no longer smiling. Vandana looked back at Octavia as if looking at something far away. For a moment Octavia imagined that this stranger saw everything she saw—Ursula's suffering, and Octavia's refusal to acknowledge it. She imagined this stranger forgiving her.

"It's a great place to hide," Vandana had said. A part of Octavia wanted to hide too. She quieted it. She got up and opened the curtains. The terrible red light came in, like the world they'd known bleeding out an ugly and long death, beyond the salvation of individuals, special abilities or not. But wasn't it beautiful too. The bougainvillea blooms had never been so saturated. They were dripping with color. And the leaves of the fig tree, this impossible child's-marker blue. Perhaps—perhaps, like her visitor, the world was only revealing a secret of her nature, her hidden alien sky, indifferent to the dramas of the self, and you were to meet her with love, not fear. Octavia sat down beside Vandana. The yellow pinprick of the sun rose behind its red curtain, casting bright glowing shapes that changed and moved upon the floor. The women sat in silence, together, watching.

Acknowledgments

Many books and writers directly and indirectly shaped the writing of this book. These works influenced the text notably: *On Photography* by Susan Sontag, *Family Lexicon* by Natalia Ginzburg, Grace Paley's short stories "Wants" and "A Conversation with My Father." The lines read aloud by Gugu in "Self-Portrait with Ghost" are from *Chinese Painting* by James Cahill, on fifth-century artist Zong Bing's "Preface on Painting Landscape." The audiobook Chenchen listens to in "In the Event" is based on *Death's End* by Liu Cixin. "The Odd Women" takes its title from Vivian Gornick's *The Odd Woman and the City*. Vandana, Ursula, and Octavia are named after Vandana Singh, Ursula K. Le Guin, and Octavia Butler. I am grateful to all these writers and works.

I am grateful to my brilliant friends, whose works have also shaped me, for reading some or all of these stories with care and intelligence: Shruti Swamy, Mimi Lok, Susanna Kwan, Yalitza Ferreras, Sunisa Manning, C Pam Zhang, Edyson Julio, Swati Khurana, Rachel Khong, Natalie So, Simon Han; to Jin Auh, Jessica Bullock, Elizabeth Pratt, Maggie Aschmeyer, and the Wylie team; to Kate Nintzel and the people at Mariner: Laura Cherkas, Maureen Cole, Molly Gendell, Jeanie Lee, Mumtaz Mustafa, Ryan Shepherd, Liate Stehlik, and many more—this book would not exist without you. To my family and friends, and to Neel, for everything that is more important than writing.

Credits

Grateful acknowledgment is made for permission to reprint the following.

"With Feeling Heart" originally published in *The Margins* as "Self Portrait with Feeling Heart."

"In the Event" originally published in *The Threepenny Review*, and reprinted in *The Best American Short Stories 2020* and *The Pushcart Prize XLV: Best of the Small Presses*.

Excerpt from *Self-Portrait* by Celia Paul. Copyright © 2020 by Celia Paul. Used by permission of the Wylie Agency LLC.

Excerpt from *Family Lexicon* by Natalia Ginzburg, translated by Jenny McPhee. Copyright © 1963, 1999, 2010 by Giulio Einaudi Editore, s.p.a., Turin. Translation copyright © 2017 by Jenny McPhee. Reprinted by permission of Einaudi and New York Review Books.

Excerpt from "Wants" from *The Collected Stories* by Grace Paley. Copyright © 1994 by Grace Paley. Reprinted by permission of Farrar, Straus and Giroux.

Excerpt from *Chinese Painting* by James Cahill. Copyright © 1960, 1977 by James Cahill. Reprinted by permission of James Cahill estate.